Dear Reader,

After more than twenty-five years, Silhouette Romance® is leaving the shelves, and next month will be the last month of publication. However, we are thrilled to announce that the authors you know and love—whose stories have made you laugh and cry—have a new home at Harlequin Romance®!

Each month Harlequin Romance will be on the shelves with six new titles. You'll find your favorite authors from Silhouette Romance, and some exciting new names, too! Most importantly, Harlequin Romance will be offering the kinds of stories you love—and more! From royalty to ranchers, bumps to babies, big cities to exotic desert kingdoms, these are emotional and uplifting stories from the heart, for the heart!

So make a date with Harlequin Romance—we promise it will be the most romantic date you'll make!

Happy reading!

Kimberley Young
Senior Editor

Please address questions and book requests to:
Silhouette Reader Service
U.S.: 3010 Walden Ave., P.O. Box 1325, Buffalo, NY 14269
Canadian: P.O. Box 609, Fort Erie, Ont. L2A 5X3

CLAIRE BAXTER

Like many authors, Claire Baxter tried several careers before finding the one she really wanted. She's worked as a PA, a translator (French), a public relations consultant and a corporate communications manager. She took a break from corporate communications to complete a degree in journalism and, more importantly, to find out whether she could write a romance novel—a childhood dream. Now she can't stop writing romance. Nor does she plan to give up her fabulous lifestyle for anything. Claire grew up in Warwickshire, England, but she now lives in the beautiful city of Adelaide in South Australia, with her husband, two sons and two dogs. When she's not writing, she's either reading or swimming in her backyard pool—another childhood dream—or even reading in the pool. She hasn't tried writing in the pool yet, but it could happen. Claire loves to hear from readers. If you'd like to contact her, please visit www.clairebaxter.com

This is Claire's first novel. Her future books will be published in Harlequin Romance®—the home of pure romance and pure emotion!

Falling
for the
Frenchman

CLAIRE
BAXTER

SILHOUETTE *Romance*®

Published by Silhouette Books

America's Publisher of Contemporary Romance

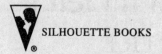

SILHOUETTE BOOKS

ISBN-13: 978-0-373-19847-4
ISBN-10: 0-373-19847-7

FALLING FOR THE FRENCHMAN

First North American Publication 2007

Visit Silhouette Books at www.eHarlequin.com

Printed in U.S.A.

A few words from Claire on
FALLING FOR THE FRENCHMAN

With famous wines, a lively heritage and more than fifty wineries, the Barossa Valley is everything you'd expect of Australia's oldest wine region. When my husband surprised me with a romantic weekend in the Barossa to celebrate our wedding anniversary, we drove among vines tended by the region's 500 grape-growing families—many of them sixth-generation—and I recalled a news report on an attempted winery takeover by a multinational conglomerate.

Until then, I hadn't considered the effects of such a takeover on a community steeped in tradition. This was where the story of Beth and Pierre began. In real life, these takeovers don't always have a happy ending, but I was able to make sure this one did—which is lucky, because I grew very attached to Beth and Pierre, and believe both of them deserved their happy ending. I hope you do, too.

To Colin, my husband, for believing in me, making me laugh and bringing balance to my life.

CHAPTER ONE

BETH LOWE was startled from her unhappy daydream by her friend and employee, Tasha Mills, bouncing through the office door.

'Today's the day we meet the boss, *n'est ce pas?*' Tasha said. 'How do you like my French?'

Beth placed her pen on the pile of cheques she should have been signing and frowned. 'If you mean Pierre Laroche, he's not my boss.' She glanced at her watch. 'And he should be here any minute now.' She leaned back, the old leather chair creaking. 'He speaks English, you know.'

'So I guessed. But it won't hurt to wow him with my linguistic ability, will it? All eight phrases.' Tasha perched on the corner of Beth's desk. 'Why didn't you meet him at the airport? You want to make a good impression, don't you?'

Anger bubbled inside Beth and she made a conscious effort to maintain her outward calm. Did she want to impress Pierre Laroche? Impale him might be nearer the mark. Ten years earlier he'd stolen her heart—then broken it. Now he was back in her life, but this time he wasn't interested in her heart. It was her winery he wanted to steal. And she had to be professional around him. She had to act like the capable business-person she purported to be.

Tasha examined her nails while she waited for an answer, and Beth took a deep breath. She couldn't expect Tasha to understand. She hadn't told her friend about her disastrous relationship with Pierre—the biggest mistake of her life. And she hadn't told her the truth behind his imminent visit either. She cleared her throat. 'I want to impress him with my management ability, not my driving skills,' she said.

Tasha shrugged. 'Point taken. Still, I'd have thought… Oh, hey, I'm sorry if I seem insensitive. I know you're cut up about the takeover. But it's done. *C'est la vie.*' She grinned and made a flourish with one hand. 'But seriously, you did your best to prevent it, and it wasn't your fault the Board voted the wrong way.'

Not her fault? She wasn't so sure. There must have been something she could have said to sway the directors to her side, to persuade them selling L'Alliance a controlling stake in Lowland Wines was a bad move. She'd tried to convince them to reject the takeover bid out of hand. Failing that, they could have accepted a lower—and unconditional—offer from a Canadian consortium. But, no, they'd been lured by the big dollars offered by the huge French conglomerate. Now her job was on the line—along with the dream her father had entrusted to her.

'Do you know anything about him?'

She refocused her eyes on Tasha. 'What?'

'This guy—Pierre. Do you know what he's like?'

'Um…' Beth stood and walked to the window. 'No.' It wasn't a lie. Exactly. He'd shown himself to be very different from the man she'd thought she'd known. And besides, a lot could have happened in the ten years since she'd last seen him. She didn't know anything about the person he'd become.

She stared at the uniform rows of vines curving with the contours of the Barossa Valley, practically unchanged since her childhood. This had been her father's office, and she'd spent hours by this window, waiting for him to finish work and walk back to the house with her. She loved the view. It almost always had the power to relax her. But how much longer would it be hers? How long did she have before L'Alliance decreed she was more of a liability than an asset and moved her aside?

Beth tensed as a white car came into view. A taxicab. 'I think he's here,' she murmured.

Tasha dashed to the window, all but nudging her aside. 'Shall I go and meet him—show him in here?'

Beth looked at Tasha's sparkling eyes. She clearly hadn't picked up on Beth's ambivalence towards their visitor. Stifling a sigh, she nodded. 'Okay, Tash. You do that.'

'How do I look?' Tasha finger-combed her short black curls.

'Beautiful. As always.' Resisting the urge to smooth her own hair, Beth turned back to the window. The view hadn't worked its magic today. Her turmoil was too deeply entrenched. She sucked in a steadying breath. She'd had a decade to forget Pierre but the memories

had persisted. Vivid and painful. Invading her dreams.
Now he would be on her territory, but she wouldn't
have the advantage. He'd still have that. Once again, he
was in a position to hurt her.

She heard Tasha giggling and grimaced. He'd won
over her friend already. Straining hinges groaned as the
heavy door swung open and, rigid with anticipation, she
listened to their footsteps on the polished timber floor.

'Hello, Babette.'

Not that name. His voice reverberating inside her, Beth
clenched her stomach muscles to hold back the nausea,
pasted a professional smile on her face and turned.

'Pierre, I didn't realise you'd arrived.' She ignored
Tasha's raised eyebrows and tried to focus on the tall
businessman in front of her—difficult, because he kept
morphing into the twenty-year-old she'd loved. In an
instant she took in everything about him. His dark brown
hair, shorter, but still long enough to curl over the collar
of his immaculate white shirt. His strong-featured face,
some age lines, but otherwise unchanged. His dark,
almost black eyes. They'd always intrigued her. Even in
the young Pierre they'd seemed wise beyond their years.

But she refused to be intrigued by them now. She
gathered her defences. She had to be able to look at him
without melting into mush. She had to work with him,
for God's sake.

There was something about him she didn't recognise. Something new. It was in his stance, his body
language. Arrogance? Self-assurance? Or was it just
that he didn't want to be there? She couldn't blame him
for that. She swallowed. If she didn't sit down, her

knees would give way—and give *her* away. She took a shaky step towards her chair, the old leather chair that had been her father's.

'Please have a seat, Pierre,' she said, ashamed of the slight tremor in her voice. 'Tasha, perhaps you could arrange some coffee for us?'

'Sure. And some Tim Tams?' Tasha flashed a smile at Pierre as he settled his tall, wide-shouldered body in the visitor's chair, blatant admiration pouring from her eyes. 'They're chocolate biscuits,' she explained. 'Beth's weakness.'

Beth glared at Tasha over Pierre's head. She didn't want him to know she had *any* weaknesses, however small. 'No biscuits, thank you.'

Pierre smiled at Tasha as she left the office, then straightened his face before turning back to Beth. *She* hadn't smiled. Unless you could count that slight curve of the lips she'd greeted him with. Not that it surprised him. If she'd welcomed his arrival he would have known it was an act. But then, she was good at acting as he recalled.

He rubbed a hand along his jaw. It had been a long flight, and he felt the slight rasp of stubble against his palm. Maybe he should have put off this first meeting till he'd freshened up. 'Babette—'

'Please,' she said, holding up a hand. 'Call me Beth.'

He nodded, remembering the day his father had first used the name he associated with her. The day she'd arrived at the Laroche family home as a bubbly, green-eyed nineteen-year-old.

She looked up, and those unusual ivy-green eyes pierced him. 'I'm sorry—I interrupted you,' she said. 'What were you going to say?'

He swallowed, dragged his mind back to the present and gazed at her. She didn't look so different from the last time he had seen her, ten years ago. 'You've cut your hair.'

Her eyes opened wide and she lifted one hand to tug at the flicked-out ends resting on her shoulders. What was he thinking, making a personal remark? Must be the jet lag messing with his mind. That, combined with the shock of seeing how little she'd changed. He straightened his tie, then cleared his throat.

'I'm sorry,' he said. 'I shouldn't have commented.' Shouldn't even have thought about it. Reminiscing over old times had no place in his plan.

This was his first time in Australia—a country he'd managed to avoid to date. But he hadn't been able to refuse this assignment. His boss had made that very clear. Besides, he was sure he could handle it. He was a thirty-year-old executive with plenty of life experience, not an impressionable twenty-year-old.

Once he'd had some sleep he'd be back on top of his game. Then he'd complete the job he'd been sent to do, and leave. As quickly as possible.

'Did you have a good flight?'

He started as Beth spoke again, in that throaty but gentle voice with the wide vowels of her Australian accent. As in the past, it sent a ripple of awareness through him, and he couldn't allow that. Steeling himself, he jerked his thoughts back to reality. He was there to do a job, however distasteful. He had to keep his mind on business.

'Yes, thank you. Long, of course, but it gave me an opportunity to study the accounts.'

The accounts. That was more like it, Beth thought. Business questions she could handle. She couldn't believe he'd mentioned her hair. She'd only recently had it cut, in an attempt to overhaul her image. To make herself look more like a managing director. But it had been a mistake. She'd wanted a sophisticated style, something that looked efficient, businesslike, but she'd ended up looking even younger and sillier.

Tasha edged her way into the office, carrying a tray, and Beth made space for it on her desk. 'Thanks, Tash.'

She reached for the cup Tasha held out to her and noted her friend's fresh lipstick. So that was what had taken so long. Not that she needed it. She was striking without make-up. If only *she* looked more like Tasha, her hairstyle wouldn't matter. She'd be more confident. People would know she meant business just by the way she carried herself.

'Pierre.' Tasha handed him the second cup. 'I must say I'm disappointed,' she said. 'I expected a sexy French accent, but you hardly have an accent at all.'

Beth saw his eyebrows shoot up. Tasha was nothing if not forthright.

'I've spent a lot of time in America,' he said with a shrug. 'My current office is in California.'

'Ah, that explains it, I suppose. Well, if you feel like reverting to your native tongue, I have a fairly good grasp of the basics.' She smiled. 'And Beth can speak French fluently, you know.'

He nodded. 'I remember.'

With a puzzled glance from Pierre to Beth, Tasha asked, 'Have you two met before?'

'Yes,' Beth said quickly. 'A long time ago. I'll bring Pierre out to the cellar door later. Don't let us keep you.'

She winced at Tasha's expression, and was relieved when she left the room without further comment. She didn't want to answer awkward questions, and she had no idea what Pierre might say. As the door closed, she caught him attempting to stifle a yawn.

'I was going to ask what you'd like to discuss first, but I guess you'd like to go to your hotel and rest. I expect you've booked a room at the resort complex?'

He shrugged. 'My office said *you* would take care of those arrangements.'

They could have told her. 'You don't have a reservation?'

'Not as far as I know.'

Her mind raced. With a golf tournament going on in the valley, the resort would most likely have filled up by this late stage, and it was the only local hotel of any note.

'If you'll excuse me, I'll make a quick call.' She lifted the cordless phone and swivelled her chair a quarter-turn away while she dialled a number. Within seconds she received the response she'd expected. No rooms available.

She knew of plenty of self-contained cottages dotted around the valley, but it seemed the height of bad

manners to shuffle him off to one of those. Especially
when their own guesthouse stood empty. She couldn't
afford to give him an extra excuse to disapprove of her.
He had enough as it was.

'No luck there,' she said, swinging back. 'But it's not
a problem. We can offer you accommodation here. You
can stay in The Barn.'

'The *barn*?'

She bit her lip to hold back a laugh as she realised
how it must sound. 'It's not a barn any more,' she explained. 'It's a house we hire out to guests. It's perfectly
comfortable.'

'I see,' he said. 'Perhaps if you called it something
else, it might be more popular?'

'It's very popular.' She damped down her defensive
reaction. 'We had a last-minute cancellation or it
wouldn't be free. I'll take you up there.'

She stood and led the way from the office, pausing
when she saw the large suitcase standing near the door.
The Barn was only a short walk from the winery itself,
but all uphill, and the case looked heavy. 'If you like,
I'll drive that up later, when I bring your food,' she said.

'No need. I'll carry it.'

She shrugged and continued into the brilliant South
Australian sunshine. They'd only walked for a couple
of minutes when she heard Pierre mutter a few words
in French. Looking over her shoulder, she saw he'd
stopped and removed his dark suit jacket. He tossed it
onto his suitcase, loosened his tie, and rolled up his
shirtsleeves to his elbows.

Beth felt a thud in her chest at the sight of him in his

white cotton shirt. His body was more muscular than when she'd known him before, if the way he filled out the shirt was anything to go by. He'd always had a tall and broad shape, but he'd been quite skinny, with very little flesh on the bones. Now he'd grown into his body.

'I didn't expect it to be so warm, so early in the day,' he said.

She shook off the strange sensation that had gripped her. Telling herself to remember who he was and what he was there for, she began walking again.

'This is quite mild. And we're hoping it stays like this. Last year we had a ten-day heatwave at the start of vintage and the vines shut down. Then the rest of it was cool, so it took a while for the sugar levels to get up.'

He caught up with her.

'Will you be here for the vintage?' she asked.

He shrugged. 'I don't think this job will take long.'

The simple truth, but so cold. Her father's dream, her own life, both reduced to the status of a job that could be disposed of quickly. They continued in silence for a little while.

'What did you mean by saying you'd bring food later?' he said.

She started. She'd been immersed in her own miserable thoughts. 'Oh, I prepare a basket of food for breakfast and lunch. All local produce. There's a fully-equipped kitchen in the barn. As for dinner, most people…'

Most people would drive to a local restaurant for dinner. But, apart from having no transport, he wasn't most people. He had the power to dictate her future. It wouldn't be wise to alienate him on his first night by leaving him to his own devices. She had to behave as if he was any other executive from head office. Reluctantly, she accepted what she had to do. 'As for dinner, you're welcome to come to the house.'

He looked surprised, but after a moment he nodded. 'Thank you. I'm not used to fending for myself.'

Her stomach lurched, and already she regretted the invitation. She certainly didn't want to be alone with him. 'Tasha will be there,' she said, mentally crossing her fingers that she'd be free.

He nodded again.

'And Maurice. My…the man I'm dating.'

There. She'd said it. She sucked in a breath. She'd wanted him to know she hadn't spent ten years pining for him. Because she hadn't. She'd got on with her life. He didn't react, but she felt his gaze on her as they walked the last few metres.

'Here it is,' she said, gesturing towards The Barn. 'Most of the original barns in the valley were built in a German style, but this one is unusual in that it's in a French style—as you can see.'

He acknowledged what she'd said, and she unlocked the door, pushed it wide open and stepped inside. As always, she smiled with satisfaction as she looked around the rectangular space at the mellow stone walls, the comfy cream sofas, the refectory table and chairs. Behind the table, a large open-plan kitchen of stainless steel and pale granite gleamed. She turned as Pierre entered, and waited for his eyes to adjust to the softer light.

'What do you think?' she asked.

'Very nice.'

She indicated a door at one end. 'There's a staircase behind there. It leads to two big bedrooms, each with its own bathroom, so take your pick.'

He walked past her into the centre of the room. 'It's better than I expected.'

She made her way back to the door, where she paused. 'My house is over there,' she said, pointing down the hill. 'Behind the winery buildings. We'll see you around seven o'clock for dinner. Dress casual. Okay?'

'Okay.'

She stepped over the threshold and hurried down the hill.

As soon as Beth had left, Pierre placed the suitcase on the floor and strode back to the doorway. He watched her follow the dusty track. Even with the weight of managing her father's winery on her shoulders, she had a spring in her step. Though she wasn't a girl any more, she had a child-like vulnerability about her. No wonder Frank Asper didn't believe her capable of running the business.

A swirling breeze caught the light fabric of Beth's floaty skirt and whipped it taut against her body. He tensed, clamping down on the surprising surge of heat through his veins. It felt a lot like desire. But it couldn't be. Not for this woman. Not after so long. And not after what she'd done to him.

He turned from the door, slamming it behind him, and swore at his boss for sending him to Australia. If he could have talked his way out of it he would have done, but Frank had been adamant, insisting the job needed

his talent. He didn't see why. It looked to him as if
Frank had already made up his mind about Beth. And
she could be stubborn. He remembered that. He didn't
think there was much chance of her agreeing to change
the way she ran the business. She ran it her father's way
and, unless she could be made to see sense, would
continue to do so. Until she was fired.

He shouldn't pre-empt his investigation, but instinct
told him he'd be recommending Beth be moved aside
for a more experienced manager. For Lowland Wines to
earn its place in the company stable it needed someone
who understood the international wine market. A
ruthless operator. It was a simple matter. If she couldn't
do the job, or wouldn't do it the way they wanted her
to, she'd have to go.

He sighed. At least Frank had promised this would
be the last overseas assignment he had. He was in line
for a promotion that would see him based permanently
at head office in France. And he was glad of it. He was
sick of travelling, tired of living out of a suitcase, and
besides, all his plans for the future depended on him
having a stable home base. He wanted to get on with his
life. So the sooner he submitted his report on Lowland
Wines, the better.

CHAPTER TWO

BETH strode across the lawns towards one of the ninety-year-old cottages. This one they'd converted into the winery's cellar door sales outlet.

Thank God that was over, she thought. His whole visit would be difficult to deal with, but nothing could be as excruciating as their first meeting after so long. For her, anyway. She hadn't seen any sign that he'd suffered, yet her pulse was only now slowing to its natural rhythm.

He was every bit as good-looking as she remembered. More so. But the shy, artistic young man had become a pragmatic executive. Was any of the old Pierre buried beneath that efficient exterior?

Not that she cared.

The rough-hewn red-gum tables and benches arranged on the grass outside the cottage being unoccupied, Beth peered through the glass door to check for customers before entering. At the sound of the door opening Tasha glanced over her shoulder from a display of wine. 'Oh, it's only you.'

'Charming,' Beth said as she settled on a high stool

and leaned her elbows on the counter. 'You have to come to dinner tonight at my place. Please say you can.'

Tasha walked around the counter and sat on another of the stools. 'Why?'

'Because I've invited Pierre to dinner, and I'll ask Maurice, so I need you to balance the numbers.'

'Oh? So, *now* you want me?'

Beth flinched. 'I'm sorry about rushing you out of the office earlier. Forgive me?'

'Hmm. *Je ne sais pas.*' She stuck her nose in the air in a pensive pose.

'Oh, come on, Tash. We'll have your favourite dessert.'

Tasha scratched her cheek and her mouth twisted into a smile. 'Want me to bring the wine?'

'Yes, please. You'd better make it the good stuff.'

'Beth Lowe, I'm surprised at you. Lowland Wines doesn't produce anything else.'

Beth flapped a hand in the air. 'You know what I mean, Tash. The *best* stuff.'

'So why didn't you tell me you'd met Pierre before?'

Beth sighed. 'It was a long time ago. His father, Thierry, was Dad's friend, and I stayed with the Laroche family to learn winemaking French-style.'

'I knew you'd spent time in France, but you didn't tell me about him.'

'There was nothing to tell.'

Tasha stared at her and she squirmed.

'Okay,' Tasha said, letting her off lightly. 'You say Maurice is coming to dinner?' She rolled her eyes as she spoke.

'Don't disrespect the man I'm going out with.'

Tasha sighed. 'You and Maurice aren't right for each other, so put him out of his misery and tell him so.'

'You think going out with me makes him miserable?'

'Not just him. Seeing you with Maurice is like watching a non-contact sport. Anyway,' Tasha said, 'if you've no interest in Pierre, you won't mind me…um…flirting with him, will you?'

Beth stared at her hands where they were splayed on the red-gum counter and forced a smile to her face. She did mind. Very much. But, having chosen to say nothing about their shared past, she could hardly complain.

'It's none of my business what you get up to in your own time,' she said, with feigned lightness. 'But do me a favour and make sure he knows you're a good cellar door sales manager, okay? I don't want him thinking all you do is flirt with the customers.'

Tasha grinned. 'Deal.'

Beth thought about Maurice as she went back to her office. It was handy to have someone to call on when she needed a date, but Tasha was right. They didn't have a real relationship. After years of wondering why Pierre hadn't wanted her, Maurice's attention had given her back some self-esteem, and she was grateful for that. But gratitude wasn't enough.

She pushed open the office door and almost collided with her cellar manager. She blew out a breath. 'John, you nearly gave me a heart attack. Were you looking for me?'

He nodded. 'About those barrel orders?'

Beth gladly shifted gear to winery business, shelving thoughts of Maurice. And Pierre.

* * *

When Pierre woke, he reached for his watch, which he'd left on the bedside table, and was startled to see he was running late for dinner. He'd slept solidly for several hours. Maybe it hadn't been such a good idea to go to bed, he thought. Now he'd struggle to adjust his body clock to local time. But it was probably something to do with not sleeping for several nights prior to the trip. Ever since Frank had told him where he had to go and what he had to do.

He showered, shaved, and unpacked some clothes. Casual, he reminded himself, and dressed in dark blue denim jeans and a coffee-coloured polo shirt.

When he was ready, he locked the door with the key Beth had left and set off down the hill. For the first time he took in the scenery, and it gave him a jolt to see its similarity to the region where he'd grown up. Not the same. For one thing the trees were different—eucalypts predominated in the Barossa—but, just like the Rhone Valley, vines cloaked all visible ground. It certainly resembled Europe more closely than the Californian country he'd grown used to in recent times, and that surprised him.

He found his way to Beth's house, skirting the modern winery buildings and following a dirt track to the front door. It didn't look as old as the barn, nor the cottage where Beth's office was located, but by no means could it be called a modern building. A long, low, single-storey house with wrap-around verandahs, shaded by tall gum trees. He stepped up to the door and knocked.

When there was no answer, he tried again, and this time he heard footsteps. As Beth flung open the door, he saw her expression change. Clearly she'd expected someone else. Her boyfriend, perhaps? Her broad grin faded to a polite smile of welcome. And for some inexplicable reason it hurt.

'Pierre. You're early.'

He frowned. 'I thought I was late.'

'It's only six-thirty. But come in—it's fine.'

'I set my watch to local time,' he said as he stepped over the threshold. 'It says seven o'clock.'

'I guess you set it to Sydney time. South Australia is half an hour behind Sydney.'

'Oh. I'm sorry.'

'No problem. I'm preparing some salads. So, if you like, you can sit in the kitchen while I work. Or you can have a seat outside.'

She started to walk along the passageway and he followed her, finding himself in a large, bright kitchen. He pulled out a chair from the table and sat while Beth stood at the kitchen bench, chopping salad vegetables.

'Is there anything I can do to help?' he asked. 'Open wine, for instance?'

'Tasha's bringing the wine.'

He raised his eyebrows. 'You don't have any here?'

'Yes, of course. But we thought you'd like to try the premium Shiraz, which is our signature red, and a few others. Tasha will know what to choose.'

He nodded. A good time to start learning about the business. The sooner the better. He leaned back and looked around the room. It had a homely ambience, but no countrified clutter. Beth's decorative style was bright and colourful. Abstract paintings lined the walls of the dining area, and he wondered whether they were her work.

She'd been keen on art when he'd known her. It was one of the many things they'd had in common. And it had been a trip to the Louvre in Paris that had led to the defining moment of their relationship. They'd been so absorbed in the art, and in each other, that they'd lost track of time and had to stay overnight. In a cheap hotel. In a single room. A single bed. He shook his head. He definitely couldn't think about that now. Nor did he want to.

'Don't you like them?'

Beth's voice startled him. 'What?'

'You're shaking your head at the paintings. I know you were never a fan of abstract—'

'No, no—I mean…' He took another look at the artwork he'd stared at without seeing. 'They are…interesting,' he said, tilting his head to one side. 'Your work?'

'Yes.'

'I thought so. They have your energy.'

He saw her freeze in the act of grating a carrot, and he gave himself a mental slap. If she remembered those days half as well as he did, she'd recall him praising her energy. Her *joie de vivre*, her easy laughter. With her Australian sense of adventure she'd endeared herself to all his family, but she'd had a more devastating effect on him. The enthusiasm with which she lived her life had left him breathless…and in love.

'I think I'll wait outside,' he said.

It had been a big mistake to come to Australia. He hadn't mastered his feelings as well as he'd thought, and that could pose a problem. He had a job to do, and he couldn't afford to be distracted. He pushed away from the table and walked through the open doors, across the wide verandah and down to the lawn.

Beth watched him go, then exhaled. Damp from the shower, his hair looked darker. Clean-shaven and wearing a subtle aftershave that lingered behind him in her kitchen, he exuded masculinity. He seemed even more good-looking in his jeans and stretchy shirt than in his business suit. Possibly because he'd been in casual clothes when she'd fallen in love with him.

No one had ever made her feel as good about herself. No one had appreciated her point of view or her company as much. Where other people had seen restlessness, he'd seen vitality. He'd loved the real her. Or so she'd thought.

Just when he'd built up her confidence, and she'd found the courage to be herself, he'd rejected her. And the pain had been so much worse because she'd believed all he'd said.

She slammed the carrot on the chopping board. She shouldn't think about the past. It had absolutely no relevance to what was happening now. She had to treat Pierre with the respect due to a representative of the new owners of the winery. She had to be polite. It would be sensible to cultivate a co-operative atmosphere. It was the only way she'd have a chance of gaining his support with his boss. Their boss.

Her personal feelings had to remain hidden. She couldn't and wouldn't allow them to jeopardise her professional relationship with the man who had the power to tear down her father's dream and toss her aside.

She quickly assembled the salad and popped the bowl into the fridge. She had to check the meat, then she'd be finished. Outside, she lifted the lid of the kettle barbecue and savoured the scent of rosemary and garlic. She closed the vents on the barbecue before replacing the lid and leaving the meat to rest.

'It smells good.'

She swung around. She hadn't heard Pierre approaching. 'It's nothing special,' she said. 'I'm not a great cook.'

He shrugged. 'You have to be better than me. I can't cook at all.'

'I get by.' She remembered his mother and her reluctance to let anyone into her kitchen. It wasn't surprising he hadn't learnt to cook there, but what about later? Had he relied on restaurants since leaving home?

She walked up the steps to the verandah. 'What do you think of the barn? Will it be suitable?' she asked.

'Yes, thank you. Where can I find the phone line so I can check my e-mail?'

'I'm afraid there isn't one. Most of our guests like to get away from work when they stay there. Do you need to connect tonight? You could use my office if you do.'

'No, but tomorrow morning?'

'Sure thing.' Beth heard a car door slam and glanced towards the house. 'I think one of the others has arrived. Before they come in…' She bit her lip. 'I haven't told anyone why you're here. I mean, they think you're doing a routine review for the new owners. Only the Board knows about the offer being conditional and my job… Well, you know what I mean.'

'I understand. And…' He shot a glance at the open doors. 'I gather you haven't told anyone about our previous acquaintance either?'

She shook her head. 'Only that I learnt winemaking from your father.' She smoothed out her expression before moving towards the door. 'Have a seat.' She indicated the table covered by a bright cloth.

Beth found Tasha in the kitchen, opening wine, and did a double-take. Her friend was dressed to impress in a low-cut skin-tight top and leather mini-skirt. She had the body to carry off the outfit, and Beth couldn't blame her for making the most of it. Eight years had passed, Beth thought, since Tasha's husband had died, and she'd become desperate for male company.

'Hey, kiddo,' Tasha said. 'Is Pierre here already?'

'Yes. He was on Sydney time, but we've sorted that out.'

Tasha chuckled, and her dangly earrings rattled. 'What about Maurice?'

'Not yet, but you know what he's like.'

'Thoughtless?'

'I meant *busy*.'

'Oh, right,' Tasha said, picking up the tray she'd set the wine on.

Beth took two salad bowls from the fridge and followed Tasha outside. She arrived in time to see Pierre's eyes flicker over Tasha as she bent to place the tray on the table. He greeted Tasha with cool politeness, but Beth felt a stab of jealousy—an emotion she hadn't experienced for a very long time.

The front door banged and she hurried back into the house.

'Hi, Beth. Got your message,' Maurice called as he strode down the passageway. 'Where's this bigwig from France?' he asked, in his normal booming voice.

'Shh, he'll hear you.'

'So?' He gave her a peck on the cheek and continued on his way outside. Beth grabbed the remaining salad bowl and dashed ahead of him to make the introductions.

Maurice held out his hand to Pierre. 'So, you're going to turn Beth into a model managing director, are you?'

Pierre glanced at her before responding, 'I'm here to do a routine review.'

'Right. I think she's a lost cause.' Maurice laughed. 'I mean, look at her clothes tonight.'

Beth looked down at her Indian cotton dress.

'She's an individual,' Tasha said sharply. 'And there's nothing wrong with that, Maurice.'

'Hell-oo, Tasha.' Maurice smiled. 'I see you're showing off the winery's assets.' He waved a hand towards the wine, but his eyes didn't leave her cleavage.

Beth turned from the table, glad of the excuse of collecting the meat from the barbecue. She returned, carrying a platter.

'Whoa,' Maurice said. 'Making an effort, aren't you, Beth?'

'It's only lamb.'

Tasha distracted Maurice by pouring wine for him.

'Ah, now, this is a treat,' he said. 'I don't normally merit opening the Century Hill Shiraz.'

'This is our award-winning classic dry red,' Tasha

said as she filled Pierre's glass. 'A blend of Grenache, Shiraz and Mourverdre. When Beth's father first started to produce it, in the mid-eighties, they were considered unfashionable varieties. But he knew what he was doing. Initially it was styled on the wines of the Rhône, but it's now considered a leading example in its own right.'

Beth watched Pierre's reaction as he took his first taste. He knew all about the wines of the Rhône. That was where his family's vineyard had been, and he'd been just as passionate about the wines produced there as she was about the Lowland range. He looked thoughtful as he considered the wine in his glass.

The small crease between his eyebrows was so familiar it produced an ache in her chest. Even ten years on, she couldn't look at him without being affected. His dark eyes turned in her direction and she looked away, hoping her thoughts hadn't been written all over her face. She didn't need him to think she still had feelings for him. Because she didn't. Not good ones, anyway.

CHAPTER THREE

PLEASED everyone had enjoyed the food, Beth sat back and smiled as Tasha mocked her own talent in the kitchen.

'I like to cook with wine,' she said with a broad grin. 'And sometimes I put it in the food too.'

As they all laughed, Beth caught Pierre's eye. She hadn't meant to, and nearly choked on her wine when he gave her the first genuine smile she'd seen since his arrival. It rocketed her straight back to the days when they'd shared private glances—and a lot more. Her chest tightened and breathing became difficult for a few moments, until she brought herself under control again.

'What's the story behind the label?' he asked, tapping an empty bottle and looking directly at her.

'Century Hill?' Beth smiled as she began the old familiar story. 'When my father bought the land to build this winery, there was already a well-established area of shiraz vines on the side of the hill where the barn is located. The owners of the land were descendants of the original settlers who had planted the vines exactly one hundred years before. Dad used the grapes from those vines in the first blend and he could tell immediately that he had some exceptional fruit on his hands. He knew then that his winery would be a success.'

Pierre watched her with such intense concentration as she spoke that his eyes seemed like dark tunnels. There was more to the story, but she'd forgotten what came next. Fine lines fanning out from the corners did nothing to detract from the effect of those eyes.

'This is our straight Shiraz,' Tasha said, taking over from Beth. 'Also made from fruit sourced from Century Hill.' She poured wine into the four glasses. 'I've brought the 2002 vintage, which is thought by many to be the best ever. It was a superb year, with an exceptionally long growing season. What do you think?'

Pierre finally withdrew his gaze from Beth's face. She lifted her glass to sip the wine and steady her stomach. With so much at stake, she had to find a way of dealing with his presence. She couldn't indulge in the luxury of behaving like a teenager. Forgetting what she was saying. What an idiot!

'You look like you work out,' Maurice said to Pierre. 'I'm a gym junkie myself. Perhaps you'd like me to sign you in as a guest at my health club? It would mean a trip to the city, of course.'

Pierre looked across the table at Maurice, and Beth knew he was searching for a diplomatic response. Maurice, with his lack of subtlety, wasn't Pierre's type. Not someone he'd choose to spend time with.

'Actually,' Pierre said after a moment, 'I don't enjoy gym work. I prefer to run. As early in the morning as possible.'

'Right. Each to his own. I can't convince Beth to join

me either. She's hopelessly addicted to yoga.' Maurice rolled his eyes.

'What's wrong with yoga?' Tasha asked. 'I've been thinking of taking it up too. Beth says it's very relaxing.'

'Exercise isn't meant to be relaxing,' Maurice said. 'It's supposed to be invigorating.' He slapped his chest, then grimaced at Pierre. 'Beth's into all sorts of hippie stuff,' he said. 'She's even started this New Age nonsense…meditation.'

'There's nothing *new* about meditation,' Beth said, more curtly than she'd intended. 'Some cultures have used it for a very long time. And anyway, it's better than sitting doing nothing—'

She stopped as she realised what she'd said. Her lips twitched and a bubble of laughter escaped. Tasha laughed, and Pierre joined in, while Maurice shook his head, unamused. He only found something funny if it was crass and juvenile. Not that she'd tried to be funny, it had just been a slip of the tongue, but still. She could only imagine how boring would life be if she didn't laugh at the little things.

Pierre had laughed.

Beth shot out of her seat. 'I'll fetch dessert,' she said, gathering plates.

She stood in front of the fridge, holding the door wide open. She stared into the fridge, but her mind's eye saw her and Pierre in Paris, laughing, sharing a joke and a bed.

'Are you all right?'

Her heart leapt and she spun around to see Tasha piling plates on the kitchen bench. She dragged her mind back to its proper place. 'Yes. Why wouldn't I be?'

Tasha's eyebrows lifted. 'You left the table in a hurry and you've been standing in front of that fridge since I came in. What's wrong?'

'Nothing. I was thinking.' She reached into the fridge and took out the Bienenstich, the German cake she'd bought for dessert.

'Mmm, you really did get my favourite,' Tasha said.

'Of course. I said I would.'

'Although if Pierre was on the dessert menu the choice would be more difficult.'

Beth dropped the cake knife she'd taken from the drawer and it clattered on the terracotta tiles. 'Tash, you have to stop saying things like that. He's here on business.'

'Hey, mixing business with pleasure might get us a favourable report.' She giggled, and carried clean glasses outside.

Beth rinsed the knife, then followed more slowly. When she arrived at the table, Tasha was pouring a deep golden wine into the fresh glasses.

'It's a Vin Santo-style dessert wine,' Tasha said, picking up the glass. 'Mmm…citrus peel and burnished wood.' She looked at Pierre. 'I've just had a thought. You should come to the winemaker's dinner we're hosting tomorrow night. You'll be able to see what the consumers think of the wines, and see what a great marketing tool the dinner is. Beth does a wonderful job.'

Beth made a dismissive gesture as she served dessert.

Maurice snorted. 'Boring. Wine is for drinking, not for discussing.' His words were slurred, and Beth narrowed her eyes as she looked across at him. Knowing Maurice, he'd managed to sneak in a few extra glasses.

'I would like to go. If it is okay with Beth,' Pierre said.

Tasha laughed. 'Of course it is.'

Beth saw they were waiting for a response from her. 'If you'd like to go, it's fine by me.' She didn't see how she could refuse. Damn Tasha for having the idea. She didn't like the prospect of spending more time with him than necessary.

'Are you married, Pierre?' Tasha asked, in an abrupt change of subject.

Beth froze with her dessert fork in mid-air. She felt him hesitate.

'Divorced,' he said, after a long moment.

Beth heard her fork hit the plate and saw it bounce off. A lump in her throat made it difficult to breathe. She coughed. 'Did you marry Arlette?' she asked, squeezing the words out.

He nodded.

Aware of both Maurice and Tasha staring at her, Beth looked away. She couldn't meet their eyes. She knew her own would be filled with pain. She stared out at the vines forming scarlet stripes as they reflected the setting sun. Of course he'd married Arlette. She'd known the classy brunette wanted him. She would have been the perfect wife for him. Sophisticated, elegant…French. Everything *Beth* wasn't. And yet, the marriage hadn't lasted.

'Any children?' Tasha prodded.

'Yes. One. A son.'

'Oh?' Tasha adopted her most sympathetic tone. 'Do you see him often?'

'Nowhere near as often as I'd like,' he said, and Beth allowed herself a glance at his shadowed face. It contorted for an instant, and she knew there was agony behind his words. 'Working in mergers and acquisitions, I'm always on the move,' he said with a shrug.

'Hang on a minute,' Maurice said. 'I might be slow, but I'm missing something here. Did you two know each other before today?' He wagged his finger from Pierre to Beth.

Beth nodded.

'Well, you could have said something.' He scowled at her. 'Why keep it secret?'

'It's not a secret,' she said.

'It's old news, Maurice.' Tasha flashed him a smile. 'Beth did some of her training with Pierre's father. I knew all about it. You probably did too, but you forgot.'

'Oh, right,' he said, making no effort to hide a yawn as he stood up. 'Well, I've had enough for tonight. I'm going to head off home. Good to meet you, Pierre.'

'Excuse me,' Beth said in the direction of her guests, before jumping up and following Maurice into the kitchen. 'You can't drive, Maurice. You've had too much to drink,' she said as soon as she'd shut the door.

'Well, that's rich. You were the one pushing wine on to us, showing off to your guest,' he said. 'Anyway, I haven't had too much. No more than Tasha, and you won't try to stop her driving, will you?'

'I would if I thought she'd had as much as you. But she barely had two glasses so she will be fine. Sleep here tonight, Maurice. Drive home in the morning.'

'No. I have an early meeting with clients tomorrow.'

'Why do we always have to have this argument?'

'Because you live here, in this god-forsaken place,

and you expect me to drive all the way out whenever you snap your fingers.'

'That's not fair!'

'Fair? I'll tell you what's not fair, Beth—'

The kitchen door opened and Tasha slipped inside, closing the door behind her again. 'Is it safe to come in?'

Maurice huffed, then swung around and marched to the front door.

'Maurice, don't go,' Beth called after him, but he slammed the front door in reply.

'You're not his mother, Beth. You can't tell him what to do,' Tasha said.

'I know I'm not his mother,' she snapped. She softened when she saw the surprise on her friend's face. 'I just don't want him to kill himself. Or someone else.'

She dashed to the front door and flung it open. Maurice was buckling his seatbelt when she reached the car. She knocked on his window, and although he rolled his eyes he wound it down.

'What now?' he barked.

She leaned down. 'Maurice, I'm serious about this. I want you to stay here. I can't go out with someone who drinks and drives.'

'I told you. I have an early meeting. Forget it, Beth. I'm going.'

'Well, then.' She straightened. 'I don't think we should see each other again.'

'Fine.' He wound up the window and, accelerating too hard, drove away.

She watched him go. She felt nothing but relief. Shaking her head, she went back inside the house.

Tasha was waiting for her. 'What happened?'

'We broke up.'

'How do you feel about that?'

Beth shrugged. 'Okay. Not bad. In fact, that was the easiest break-up ever.'

They looked at each other for a moment, then Tasha jerked her head. 'Our guest is waiting for the coast to clear and he looks done in. I think the travelling has caught up with him.'

Beth nodded and went out to the verandah. 'Would you like a coffee before you go?' she asked politely.

'If it's not too much trouble,' Pierre said.

'No trouble at all. I'll make up your breakfast basket while we wait for the coffee.'

'Not for me, Beth,' Tasha said from the doorway. 'I'd better go. I'll see you both tomorrow.' She sent a sparkling smile Pierre's way, then headed off through the house.

'Drive carefully,' Beth called to her as she disappeared along the passageway.

'Always do.'

Beth scooped coffee into the plunger jug. She guessed Pierre would like it strong. As she did. She'd acquired immunity to caffeine-induced insomnia when in France.

As she filled a breakfast basket, she thought about Maurice. Should she call him later to check he'd reached home safely? She sighed. No, he wouldn't want to hear from her, and they'd argue again. Better to make it a clean break. She was better off without him. She knew that. But the thought of being completely alone twisted her insides and left her stomach aching.

'Can I put these plates in the dishwasher?'

She jumped, and her heart thumped in her chest. 'Cripes! I had no idea you were there.'

'I'm sorry.'

She looked at him, and her heart thumped again, but she couldn't blame the shock this time. She could never have predicted that this particular man would be standing in her kitchen, talking about such mundane things as plates and dishwashers.

'Yes, you can.' She pointed at the appliance and watched as he transferred the plates from the kitchen bench to the slots.

'So, you're not completely useless in the kitchen, then?' she said, trying to keep the mood light and not notice the way his muscles moved.

'Not completely useless,' he said as he straightened up. 'But almost.'

He smiled down at her, and she held her breath as she turned away to pour boiling water into the plunger jug. Exhaling slowly, she promised herself she wouldn't get sucked in by that smile. She couldn't afford to. It was a dangerous weapon and she had to be wary of it.

'I think we'll have this inside,' she said as she placed everything they needed on a tray. She carried it to the table, where they sat, one on each side, facing each other.

'How long have you been going out with Maurice?' he asked.

She was surprised. She would have expected him to steer clear of personal topics, as she'd intended to.

'A while,' she said as she eased the plunger to the bottom of the jug.

'I know it's not my business, but he doesn't seem your type.'

Beth handed him a mug and took a sip from her own. It scorched her lips and tongue. 'Not any more, anyway.'

He raised his eyebrows in a silent question.

'We broke up.'

'I'm sorry.'

She put the mug down. 'No need to be. It wasn't serious.'

He nodded.

'What about you?' she asked. 'How long were you married to Arlette?'

It was as if a pair of shutters had closed over his eyes. 'Three years,' he said, after a moment.

'That's not very long.'

'Long enough.'

'To have a child?'

He shrugged.

'How old is he now?'

'Nine.'

She did a quick calculation. He must have married Arlette pretty darn quickly after she'd left. Something turned over inside her heart as she let the knowledge sink in.

'So, you've been apart for seven years?'

He nodded.

After a moment's silence, she opted for another topic of conversation. 'I was sorry to hear about your parents,' she said gently.

'It was a few years ago.'

'I know.' She'd always regretted not expressing her

sympathy, but hadn't known how to approach him. His parents had retired to the south of France. It had been there they'd had the car crash that killed both of them.

'It must have been a terrible shock for you.'

'But worse for Dominique.' He ran a hand through his hair. 'I had to tell her.'

She sucked in a sympathetic breath. His younger sister would have been still at school at the time, and her heart went out to her. What a dreadful thing to have to do—to tell her the parents she'd adored were dead.

In Beth's own case she'd had no one but herself to worry about when her father died. At the time, she'd bitterly regretted not having siblings. She hated being left alone. But maybe it could have been worse. She took a cautious sip of her coffee. 'Mmm, that's good,' she said.

He agreed.

'I didn't know until they died that they'd sold the vineyard. I was shocked,' she said.

Pierre's face twisted. He pushed the coffee mug away and scraped back his chair. 'It's late. I think I'd better go.'

She looked up at him. 'I'm sorry. I didn't realise the accident was still such a painful subject for you, or I wouldn't have—'

'It's not.'

Puzzled, she glanced at his barely touched coffee. What had she said? Was this about his father selling the vineyard? Had they argued? Maybe he'd refused to take over from Thierry and now regretted his stance? As she regretted not coming home to help her father when he had asked her. She knew all about remorse of that kind.

* * *

Early the next morning—very early, since he couldn't sleep—Pierre tried to shift his brain out of gear and let his feet do the work. He hadn't lied when he'd told Maurice he liked to run. Not only for the aerobic workout, but also for stress relief.

He was normally able to switch off his thoughts and concentrate on his muscles. Not this morning. Not after spending an evening with Babette—Beth, he corrected himself. She'd made it clear she didn't want him to use that name. Easier said than done. She'd been Babette to him for ten years. Every time he'd thought about her. And there had been plenty of those times, much as he'd tried to forget.

What had she been doing with Maurice? Thank God she'd finished with a man so wrong for her. She needed a man who appreciated her individuality. Who loved her for the person she was, not wanting to change a thing. She needed—

He doubled over as a cramp hit his calf. He rubbed it with both hands, then forced his heel to the ground to stretch the tight muscle.

This assignment was going to be the hardest he'd ever had. All he needed to do was make a perfunctory investigation of Beth's management methods and then write a damning report that would leave the Board no choice but to vote her out. But in order to do that he had to work with Beth. He had to remember what they'd shared every time he looked at her.

Before flying out, he'd convinced himself he could do it. That he wouldn't be susceptible to her any longer. He was too old, too experienced, too tough to fall for her again. But the problem was, he didn't have to fall for her again because he'd never got over her in the first place.

Pierre straightened and began to walk back. Frank had better come through with the promotion and permanent posting he'd promised him. That was the only reason he was going through with this. If not for the promotion he'd tell Frank what to do with his assignment and he'd be out of here. But the new job was crucial to his future. Without a permanent base, he didn't have a hope in hell of winning his custody case.

CHAPTER FOUR

PIERRE had thought better of wearing a suit, on account of the heat, and had dressed in light grey trousers and a white short-sleeved cotton shirt. Carrying his laptop in its case, he strode down the hill towards the winery and watched a small white truck travel along the driveway until it came to a standstill near the entrance to the office.

He turned his attention to the gnarled vines growing beside the dirt track, their foliage trellised on single wires to lift the fruit up to the sun. These were the old Shiraz vines Beth had mentioned. Her father had been right to save them. Not from a sentimental point of view, but because it had been a good business decision. The Century Hill label had a good reputation among connoisseurs, and though he hadn't tried it till the night before he could see why.

He lifted his eyes to gaze at the wider picture, and its similarity to his childhood home struck him even more forcibly. Images of life in the Laroche vineyard chased each other through his mind until he shook his head to erase them. How absurd to be having flashbacks to his childhood. And pointless. His family home was there no longer. He couldn't go back to it even if he wanted to.

He'd reached the bottom of the hill, and was about to push open the door to Beth's office when he heard her voice, bright and melodic. Then her laugh, tinkling through the narrow opening between door and frame. She was clearly having a conversation with someone she liked. She'd used to speak to him that way, and he felt a pang of regret that they were much more reserved now. Polite, not playful.

Regret was an emotion he couldn't waste time or effort on. He gritted his teeth and pushed open the door. Beth stopped speaking and looked his way. Rather than sitting behind her desk, as he'd expected, she was actually sitting *on* the desk, gripping the edge with her hands, her legs dangling.

With her hair in its new, sweet style, her laughing green eyes and a hesitant smile on her full lips, she made his chest ache.

Then he noticed her clothes. A tight, cropped T-shirt, showing her midriff, and a pair of shorts. She looked about sixteen years old, not nearly thirty. He lowered his gaze and found himself looking at her tanned, slender legs. Lower still and it came to rest on her feet. Bare feet. So very Beth. And there—

He started, and grasped the door handle in a tight fist.

There, around her ankle, the dainty gold chain he'd given her in Paris.

He knew he was staring, but how could he drag his eyes away? No doubt about it being the same chain. He could see the dainty heart-shaped design of the links, and the clasp he'd struggled to close with his not-so-dainty fingers.

Had she worn it ever since?

Did she remember where it had come from? Or was it just a habit, like wearing a wristwatch every day?

'Good morning, Pierre,' she said, sliding from the desk as she spoke. 'I'd like to introduce our vineyard manager, Clive Bauer.'

He jerked his head to his left. A man of around the same age as himself walked towards him with his hand outstretched. Mechanically, he reached out and shook the hand. So this was the guy who'd made her sound so happy.

'How're you going?'

Pierre blinked at him. 'Going where?'

Clive stared. Pierre stared back. It was an irrational emotion, but he felt jealous of the man's tanned good looks—and Beth's obvious ease with him.

'It wasn't a literal question,' Beth said. 'It means, how are you? Like *comment allez-vous*?'

Pierre made an impatient gesture. 'Of course. I knew that. I am well, thank you,' he said to Clive.

Clive grinned. A broad white smile which made him appear even more handsome. 'I'd be happy to show you around the vineyards,' he said. 'There's a hundred and fifty hectares in all. Forty-five hectares of Shiraz, forty of Semillon, twenty-five of Merlot, twenty of Cabernet Sauvignon, sixteen of Riesling, and two hectares each of Mourverdre and Grenache.' Clive took a breath. 'And then, of course, there are the growers—'

'Clive acts as our grower liaison as well,' Beth cut in. 'We have a select group of twenty-five growers, whose vineyards are scattered over the Barossa as far south as Williamstown and as far north as Ebenezer. We find the different growing conditions add complexity to the wines.'

Pierre nodded. 'Well, I'm sure you are very busy,' he said to Clive. 'I won't take up your time.' He was pleased when Clive seemed to take the hint. With a nod at Beth, he slapped his akubra on his head and loped to the door.

'See ya,' he called as the door closed behind him.

As Pierre turned to Beth, he caught a glare aimed in his direction. Her face straightened as she asked, 'You'd like to plug your laptop into the phone line?'

'Yes, please.' Was she angry that he'd interrupted her *tête-à-tête* with the handsome Clive?

She positioned a spare chair at the end of her desk, indicated the wall sockets, then sat in her own chair and focused on her computer monitor.

Beth looked up later, to see Pierre frowning at his screen. She got up and filled two glasses with water from the cooler in the corner of her office, placing one on the desk near his elbow.

'Thank you.' He glanced up. 'Beth?'

'Yes?'

'I've been looking over the business records from the last few years.'

A prickle of anticipation made its way up Beth's spine. This was it. This was where she had to start fighting for her winery. She lifted her chin. 'And?'

'You pay a lot of money for the grapes you buy from local growers.'

She looked at him for a moment. 'So?'

'So, you could save the business a significant amount by negotiating better deals with the growers.'

'Negotiating?' Her stomach clenched. She knew exactly what he meant. Her father had been through all this before. 'You mean, putting them in a position where they can't refuse to hand over their crops for a pittance?'

'It's called business, Beth. And if the growers don't want to sell more cheaply, you buy the grapes elsewhere.'

'You're kidding, aren't you?' She gave a small laugh, although she didn't see any humour in the scenario.

'No. You could buy much larger quantities for the amount of money you spend now, and then you'd be able to implement a substantial increase in production.'

'Excuse me,' she said, holding up a hand like a police officer halting traffic. 'There's no point in continuing this discussion, because it's not going to happen. No way.'

She walked around her desk and sat down, sipping at her water to calm her nerves. Pierre sighed, and her hackles rose. It was a sigh that told her he had no faith in her business acumen, that he thought her incapable of grasping the concept. And she'd heard it too often from others.

'I would have thought you, of all people, would understand,' she spat, with such venom he visibly stiffened.

'What do you mean?'

'With your background. Your father was the one who made me truly understand the importance of *terroir*. The taste of the soil, everything that makes up a particular environment.'

He leaned back and looked at her across the desk. His eyes narrowed and she couldn't read his expression.

'Nevertheless,' he said slowly, 'you are running a business here, not a hobby. You owe it to the shareholders to consider ways of increasing profit.'

'Don't be patronising.'

He looked at her for a long moment, before responding calmly, 'it was not my intention to patronise you, and I apologise if that's the impression I gave. I was simply trying to point out there are business improvements that should be made here. It's up to you whether you accept my advice.'

'Accept your advice? What you mean is, I will *have* to change the whole philosophy of this winery in order to satisfy L'Alliance. And if I refuse to destroy everything my father worked for and dreamed of I will be swept away like a pile of rubbish. That's right, isn't it?'

She saw a muscle working in his jaw. 'You knew the situation before I arrived,' he said.

'Yes, I knew the situation,' she snapped. 'I knew that L'Alliance wanted me out.'

He didn't respond, and when he turned away she knew he couldn't argue with what she'd said. When she'd spoken to Frank Asper he'd assured her she had his full support. But she'd known he had to be lying. Why else would they have placed such a condition on their offer?

She sighed. 'Pierre, you need to know that I won't compromise my father's vision for this winery. It was his dying wish for me to continue his work, and that is what I intend to do. If I fall into line with your recommendations, Lowland Wines as we know it will cease to exist.'

He stood up and stalked to the window. 'Beth,' he said with his back to her, 'there is no room in business for sentiment. If you were more experienced, you would know that.'

Biting back an emotional retort, she responded quietly, 'If that were true, my father would never have started Lowland Wines.'

Pierre half turned from the window, folded his arms across his chest and looked at her with his head tilted to the side. Her stomach lurched. He'd looked at her that way in the past. She took a deep breath and pushed away the memory. He was here for one reason and one reason only. To prove her incapable of running the winery.

'I don't believe I've heard the history of Lowland Wines,' he said. 'Tell me.'

'Well…' She considered refusing. What was the history to him? He didn't care about it. Didn't respect it. But she wouldn't lose anything by telling him how her father had started the winery. It might even help if he understood why she looked at things the way she did… But she wouldn't hold her breath.

'My father was chief winemaker for Box Tree Wines. It used to be owned by a local family, but at that time had just been swallowed up by Wesley—another international conglomerate, like L'Alliance.'

He nodded. 'I know Wesley, of course.'

'Wesley were only interested in Box Tree for its distribution network and as a base for selling their spirits in Australia. They weren't interested in its reputation as a very good wine producer. They decided to slash production at the vital time, just before the vintage.

They told Dad not to buy any grapes from the local growers.'

She took a sip of water before going on.

'Dad was devastated. He'd already done deals with the growers, and he knew if he reneged on those deals families he'd grown up with would be ruined. He refused to do it.'

She sat up a little straighter. Pride in her father's stance gave her the courage to continue on the track she'd set for herself. To stand up to L'Alliance.

'He arranged financial backing from an Adelaide company and bought the grapes himself. Then he built this winery in record time, crushed the fruit he'd bought, and Lowland Wines was born. He swore he'd always use local grapes and not cut costs by buying more cheaply interstate or overseas. He wanted the wider community of the valley to benefit from his actions. If he'd been in it for the money he would have gone about things differently from the beginning.'

Pierre gave a slight shrug. 'I see what you mean about the business being built on sentiment,' he said. 'But surely your father would want you to change if it meant the difference between you losing or retaining control?'

She considered his question for a moment before shaking her head. 'No. No, he wouldn't. He'd want me to do the right thing. Control of something you don't believe in is not worth having.'

She was tempted to add that the Pierre she'd known ten years before would have felt the same way, but bit back the comment. Too personal. She had to remain professional if she was going to influence his report at all. She pushed her chair back from the desk. Opening a drawer in one of the filing cabinets, she took out a pair of sandshoes, slipped them onto her feet and bent to tie the laces.

'I'm going for a walk around the winery,' she said as she straightened up. 'Would you like to join me?'

After introducing Pierre to Owen Lowe, her cousin and chief winemaker, Beth left them chatting while she sought out John McGill with an update on their barrel order. When she returned, she could see Pierre was totally absorbed in conversation with Owen. It had been a good idea to leave them alone. All the tension had gone from Pierre's face. He looked more relaxed than at any time since his arrival.

Whenever he spoke to her, he seemed wary. Not surprising. But if he expected her to fling recriminations at him he'd have a long wait. She was determined to maintain her dignity. If she was going to keep the winery she had to act as if she didn't care about him and what he'd done in the past.

She hovered a little way off, listening to Owen's soothing voice. He was a gentle man and a gifted winemaker. He'd also worked a vintage at the Laroche winery, but as it had been several years before Beth's own visit, Pierre would have been quite young.

'Because the fruit is everything, we opt for a minimalist approach,' Owen said softly. 'We use a neutral strain of yeast for all of our ferments, enabling natural flavour expression. If we feel the fruit lacks intensity, we will work the ferment harder to aid extraction. Usually, however, the ferment is pumped over twice daily and chilled if required.'

'How soon do you take the ferments off skins?' Pierre asked.

'Relatively early. Softness and palate structure are the aims, rather than excessive extraction. And the wine completes fermentation in oak.'

Beth strolled up to them. 'French oak, of course,' she said, smiling.

'Of course,' Pierre said, smiling back.

She clamped down on the surge of sensations that streamed through her. Her body had no right to react without her permission.

'Would you like to walk over to the cellar door now?' She kept her tone light, so as not to spoil the relaxing effect of the last half-hour.

'Yes.' He shook hands with Owen. 'Thank you for taking the time to talk to me,' he said formally.

'No problem. Any time, any time,' Owen said, clasping Pierre's shoulder with his free hand. 'You were always a natural, even as a little kid. I expected you to take over from your father.'

Pierre's face fell, but he joined Beth as she walked out into the bright sunshine. 'Owen is very knowledgeable.'

'He is, and he's a nice guy too. He worked in the Hunter Valley and the Riverland before going overseas and working on several vintages in France and Germany. Then he came back to Australia, and was in McLaren Vale when Dad asked him to take over here.'

'How long ago was that?'

'About five years. He—Dad—had been finding it too hard to manage the business side as well as the winemaking, and...'

She paused. Whenever she recalled the row she'd had with her father at that time she felt the enormous weight of having let him down. If she'd known he would only live for a short time she'd have acted differently. But, with the arrogance of youth, she'd thought she had plenty of time to join her father in the family business. It was something she'd seen happening five, even ten years in the future.

If she could go back, not only would she relieve her father of many of his work commitments, she'd spend every minute she could picking his brains, learning everything he knew about the wine industry. She'd listen to his reminiscences and treasure the word pictures he'd created when he'd talked about her mother, the love of his life, taken from him by a freak accident when Beth was only a toddler.

'He asked Owen to help him?' Pierre prompted.

She started. 'Er, not immediately. He asked me to take over the business side so he could concentrate on the winemaking himself.'

He frowned. 'But you didn't?'

She drew a deep breath. 'No, I didn't. I'd made other plans. I'd been offered a job in the Hunter Valley, and—' She swallowed. 'I took it. It was a really good offer. I didn't think I could afford to pass it up.'

'And when did you come back?'

'Not until—' She swallowed hard again. Her throat was getting tighter. 'Not until Dad was too sick to work any longer.'

They were outside the old cottage when Beth

found tears blurring her vision. She blinked them away, embarrassed.

'Sorry,' she mumbled.

'No, er, worries,' he said, attempting an Australian accent which made a smile twitch her lips. 'Do you want to sit here for a moment?' He gestured at one of the tables on the lawn.

She nodded, and slid along the bench, leaning her forearms on the solid tabletop. Pierre sat opposite.

'Tell me about it,' he said.

She knew she'd sounded callous, and she wanted to explain. Not that she deserved to be let off lightly. No one could think more badly of her than she did herself.

'You see,' she said, her voice thick with tears, 'I didn't know he was sick. He never told me. All that time he knew about the cancer, he never said a word to me. If he'd told me, I would have—' She broke off, unable to voice the regrets she carried deep inside.

He leaned forward, and for a moment she thought he would take her hand. But he didn't, and she was glad. She didn't need the extra emotions it would stir up.

'Of course you would,' he said.

How would he know? She stared into the depths of his dark eyes. She'd once thought he knew her better than anyone. She'd thought she knew him too. How wrong she'd been. She choked back a sob. The man she'd thought he was wouldn't have talked about eternal love one day and dumped her the next.

And if they hadn't really known each other back then, when they'd been so close, how could he possibly expect to know her now, ten years on?

CHAPTER FIVE

'I'M SORRY.' Beth stood up. 'I didn't intend your tour to turn gloomy. Let's go in to see Tasha.'

Tasha could be counted on to cheer her up, Beth thought as she pushed through the door. But then she saw her friend's face. White, except for two bright red blotches on her cheekbones and dark blue circles under her eyes.

'What's wrong, Tash?' She hurried around the counter to her.

Tasha didn't move. 'Migraine.'

'Oh, no. What are you doing here? Did you have it before you came to work today?'

'No…developed after I got here.'

'Well, you should have gone straight home. Do you have your medication here?'

'No. At home. Couldn't go. Been busy here this morning.' Tasha turned her eyes towards Pierre without moving her head. 'Sorry about this.'

Beth had witnessed enough of her friend's migraines to know this was going to be a bad one. 'I'll drive you home. We'll work out how to get your car back later.' She turned to Pierre. 'You won't need me for a while, will you?'

'No, but I could help with Tasha's car,' he said. 'I could follow you.'

'Oh. Well, yes, if you don't mind, that would help.'

Tasha groaned. 'Won't be able to go to the wine-maker's dinner tonight. Once I take my tablet, I'll be zonked out for about twelve hours.'

'Don't worry about it, Tash,' Beth said quickly. 'You're not indispensable, you know. I'll manage.'

'At least you won't be on your own.' Tasha bent slowly at the knees to retrieve her handbag from beneath the counter. 'Pierre will be with you.'

Beth stiffened. She'd forgotten about the invitation he'd accepted. Not a good idea. They'd be together in the car for a two-hour drive each way. And that was on top of the time they'd spend together during the day.

'Perhaps you should give it a miss.' She gave Pierre a hopeful look. 'It won't be as good without Tasha there.'

'I would still like to go,' he said with a shrug. 'But I am sorry about your headache, Tasha.'

'Not headache. Migraine,' Tasha whispered through clenched teeth.

'Would you prefer me not to go?' he asked Beth.

She flinched. 'No. Of course not. If you still want to go, it makes no difference to me.'

On the point of slamming Tasha's front door, Beth remembered her friend's head and closed it quietly.

Nothing seemed to be going according to plan. She'd thought she'd be able to avoid Pierre outside business hours—but, on the contrary, they'd be together for ages tonight, with no one else to act as a buffer.

Pierre had parked Tasha's hatchback in the free-standing carport, and seemed to be making friends with a local parrot. The brightly coloured bird, perched on a perimeter fence, whistled a clear, musical note and Pierre mimicked it.

She strolled to his side. 'I see you've met the neighbours,' she whispered.

He jumped, and the rosella flew off.

'I thought you were still inside,' he said. 'That was a beautiful bird. The sort of creature you only expect to see in a zoo.'

She nodded. 'That was an Adelaide rosella.' She pointed as another bird took off from the ground. 'There goes its mate. They're always in pairs—they mate for life.'

He stared at her, and she felt her cheeks grow hot. She hadn't intended a double meaning, but once she'd said the words…

She rushed to fill the silence. 'You should see the rainbow lorikeets. They're gorgeous. The most vivid colours, and they travel in flocks. Quite a sight. Are you ready to go?'

He nodded, and she felt the heat in her face subside. Perhaps he hadn't picked up on her embarrassment. But, with her luck, what were the chances?

It was time for lunch when they arrived back at the winery, and Beth yawned as she parked the car in her driveway. She hadn't been able to sleep more than an hour at a stretch since she'd heard Pierre was on his way. Sleep deprivation. Just when she needed to be clear-headed.

'I only packed breakfast in your basket last night,' she said. 'Do you want to come in for lunch?'

'I don't want to inconvenience you. Especially since you look so tired.'

'I'm fine. Honestly,' she said, when he looked doubtful. 'And you have to eat.'

'If you're sure.'

He followed her into the house, where she tossed her car keys on to the hall table and led the way to the kitchen.

'It won't take me long,' she called over her shoulder.

'I would like to help. I don't want you to do everything for me. It's not as if you are running a hotel.'

She turned. 'I was only going to make sandwiches.'

'Fine. What can I do?'

'Well…' She glanced around the kitchen. 'You could pour us some drinks. There's orange juice and mineral water in the fridge. I don't recommend wine, because we'll have plenty tonight.' She started to slice a crusty loaf as she spoke. 'The guests would think there was something odd about winemakers who didn't drink their own product. And, by the way, for that reason we don't drive back afterwards. I hope you won't mind staying in Adelaide?'

'Not at all.'

He found glasses without any trouble, took them to the table, and came back for plates and napkins.

'Anything else I can do?' he asked once he'd set the table.

'Um…you could slice some fruit.' She pointed in

the direction of a rock melon and a pineapple. 'If that's all right?'

He nodded and made a start.

'When you said you didn't cook at all, I thought you meant you kept out of the kitchen,' she said.

'I have until now, but—'

He paused and she glanced up. There was a strange expression on his face. What was it? Wistful?

He spotted her watching him and resumed slicing. 'I would like to learn to cook,' he said.

She stayed silent for a moment, but curiosity got the better of her. 'So why don't you?'

'I will. But for now I spend most of my time in hotels. I don't have a home, as such.'

She arranged the sandwiches on a large plate. Was that what the wistful look had been about? He wanted to put down roots? 'Where will it be when you do have one?' she asked.

He looked up, but his deep, dark eyes were guarded. 'France. I don't know exactly where yet. I should receive a permanent posting at head office as soon as this assignment…' He waved the large knife as he spoke and Beth took a step back. 'As soon as it is over.' He opened the dishwasher and slid the knife in.

'So, the sooner you decide to turf me out, the better?'

He flinched.

She could have kicked herself. 'I'm sorry, Pierre. That was unprofessional of me.'

He waved her apology away and carried the plate of fruit to the table while Beth followed with the sand-wiches. 'It's up to you whether I *turf you out*, as you say,

Beth. It depends on whether you are determined to be difficult.'

'*Difficult?*' Beth poured mineral water into her glass. 'I'm determined to maintain the integrity of this winery. Is that what you call difficult?'

'You could maintain its integrity while increasing its output.'

'No,' she said firmly. 'Quality, not quantity. That's what my father believed in and that's the philosophy I intend to uphold.'

He sighed, and took a sandwich from the plate between them.

Beth ate too. She couldn't see a way around the stalemate, which meant, no doubt, that she'd soon be out of a job. And a home. How could she bear to let it go? Perhaps it *would* be better for her to accept the demands of L'Alliance and do anything necessary to keep her position? It was what Pierre had suggested. But she wouldn't be able to run the winery her way. Or her father's way. She couldn't see herself giving in to L'Alliance. Her father hadn't given in to Wesley all those years ago, and she would hold to the same principles—no matter the personal cost to herself.

'Tell me about the dinner,' Pierre said. 'What is it all about?'

Beth looked at him and had the sense he'd read her thoughts. To add to her many other failings, she would make a lousy poker player. 'The winemaker's dinner?'

He nodded.

'Well, it's an upmarket function for people who are serious about wine. Connoisseurs and collectors, mainly. It's an opportunity to showcase our whole range throughout the night.'

'So, you stand up in front of an audience and talk about your wine?'

She nodded.

'That's brave of you.'

She narrowed her eyes, looking for sarcasm, but he seemed genuine. 'Tash and I usually split the range between us, but tonight I'll cover all of it.'

One thing she *could* do was talk about wine. She was in her element among people who were genuinely interested. 'I just hope you won't be bored.'

He shrugged. 'I don't expect so. Do you take the wine with you?'

'No, it's pre-delivered to the restaurant. I've spent time with the chef already, choosing the menu. It's all organised. And, by the way, we'll need to dress up.'

'Understood.'

Beth glanced at the clock on the kitchen wall. 'We'll have to set out at four o'clock, and I have a lot of work to do this afternoon…'

'So, you would like me to go.' He stood up and stretched his arms over his head.

Beth had to look away. 'Yes, you should go,' she said quickly. 'Or there won't be much time left to make myself beautiful.'

He smiled down at her and her stomach lurched. 'But you don't need much time,' he said. 'None, in fact.' His eyes were even darker, and even more magnetic. They held hers for a long moment.

'Thank you for the lunch,' he said suddenly, and left.

What was that? Beth closed her mouth. A bizarre bubbling started up in her stomach. What had he meant? That she was beautiful?

A throwaway compliment.

He'd never been one for cheap flattery. So, did he really think she was beautiful?

A shudder shook her, and she slapped her hands on the table.

'Get a grip,' she growled out loud. 'Don't make a fool of yourself.'

Beth had a new dress. Never sure what to wear for these functions, she sometimes thought it was the one aspect of the evening she couldn't get right. Maurice had accompanied her to the first few dinners, and he'd had something to say about every outfit she'd chosen. She'd been glad when he'd become bored and refused to accompany her. It was easier without his so-called moral support.

She unhooked a slinky black cocktail-length dress from its hanger and laid it on the bed. This time she might have found the perfect compromise between business and glamour. Would Pierre approve?

Aargh! She pulled the T-shirt over her head and flung it into the corner of the room. It didn't matter *what* Pierre thought of her dress—neither from a professional nor a personal point of view. Her shorts and underwear joined the top in the corner, and she strode into the bathroom. All she had to do was show him what a success these dinners were, and she could do that wearing a sack. She turned on the water and stepped under the massaging spray. So why was she so pleased that she had a new dress?

Once fully clothed, she sat in front of the mirror to work on her hair and make-up. She still regretted having her hair cut, but it co-operated with the hairdryer for once, and she gave the style a short blast of hairspray before it could disintegrate.

After applying more make-up than normal, she ran a critical eye over the result and shrugged. Not a bad effort, and the best she could do. She sprayed a cloud of her favourite perfume in the air and walked into it. The thought that Pierre might recognise the fragrance crossed her mind, but she dismissed it as extremely unlikely.

Picking up her handbag and car keys, Beth set off to collect Pierre from the barn—but she only made it as far as her front verandah. As she stepped through the doorway, she saw him sitting on the bench below her bedroom window.

Chaotic emotions churned her stomach. On the one hand, relief that the blind was down on the window. On the other, a longing that came from deep inside and welled up like a volcano. Nostalgia, she warned herself. Nothing but memories. Seeing him there had triggered an involuntary response. It didn't mean she still had feelings for him. It was simply that she hadn't had the opportunity to prepare for the sight.

But no amount of cold, hard logic could cool the rush of burning desire.

As he turned his head and saw her, his eyes felt like lasers, scorching her wherever their beam touched. And he looked…well, everywhere. She swallowed, and swallowed again as she tried to speak.

He stood up. 'You look stunning.'

'Thank you,' she mumbled. 'So do you.' She scanned the black suit, white shirt and yellow tie. Nice packaging—but it was memories of the body beneath it that nearly sent her into a spin.

She caught herself. She had to clamp down on this craziness before it could get out of control. 'I mean, you look very smart. That's a nice suit.'

He smiled, and her heart hammered against her ribs. Stupid. It wasn't as if they were going on a date. And he didn't mean it when he said she was stunning. He couldn't.

Remember why he's here, she told herself. *To wreck your winery.*

She would keep the words at the forefront of her mind, like a shield.

But when he held out his arm, bent at the elbow, she slipped her hand through it and the feelings that flooded over her had nothing to do with their current conflict.

They walked to her car.

'Would you like me to drive, so you can relax before your busy evening?' he asked.

'Oh, yes—thank you.' She climbed into the unfamiliar passenger seat of her Mitsubishi and settled back for the long drive.

Pierre smiled across at her as he started the engine. 'Don't look so apprehensive. I promise I'll look after it.'

'I'm not worried about the car,' she said.

'What, then?'

'Nothing. I'm not worried at all.'

Liar. She was worried that she wouldn't be able to hide her feelings. Worried that she'd say or do something to give herself away. And worried that he'd take advantage of her weakness and get her to agree to his plans for her business.

After he'd eased the car along the driveway and out into the road, they drove in silence for a while. Pierre broke it first.

'Whose idea was the winemaker's dinner?' he asked.

'We're not the only winery that holds them,' she said. 'But the Lowland Wines dinner was my idea.'

He nodded. 'You studied winemaking yourself, didn't you? Why not go into that line of work?'

'I did. I worked in the Hunter Valley for a couple of vintages, and then went to Western Australia, south of Perth, where I helped set up a new winery. When I came back to the Barossa, Owen was well and truly settled at Lowland. It was the business side of the winery that was suffering.'

She sighed. She didn't want to think about that time in detail. Not tonight.

'Anyway,' she said, 'I could ask you the same thing. Why didn't you follow in your father's footsteps instead of letting him sell the winery? It's what you always said you were going to do.'

She saw his jaw clench and his Adam's apple move up and down as he swallowed.

He exhaled, and stared straight ahead as he spoke. 'I had no choice.'

'I don't understand.'

He sighed. 'I found out my father was very bad at business. He thought if he did the right thing by other people, they'd look after him when times got tough. He was wrong. He ran the winery into the ground.'

She saw his knuckles whiten on the steering wheel and she caught her bottom lip between her teeth.

'Six generations of the Laroche family,' he said. 'And then there was nothing.'

She could feel the bitterness in his words. It made her skin prickle. She remembered how passionate he'd been about the business—how he'd talked about taking over from his father and making the best wine the Rhone Valley had ever seen.

'So, that's when he sold out to L'Alliance?'

He became pensive again. After a few moments, he jerked his head. 'Yes. Like I said, by the time I found out about the state of the business it was too late. We limped on for a few years, but in the end we couldn't do anything else.'

Something clicked into place for Beth. 'That's when you decided there was no room for sentiment in business?'

He shot her a sharp glance. 'It was a good lesson. The best.'

She stayed silent. Not only did she not want to get into another argument, but she was starting to understand why he felt the way he did. He must have been devastated by the loss of his dream. No wonder his views had been tainted. She decided to deflect the conversation from such touchy topics.

'As well as winemaking, I studied wine marketing at uni,' she said.

'Did you?' There was surprise in his voice.

'And then I did an MBA.'

'Really?'

'So I was quite happy to put those skills into practice and leave the hands-on production to Owen.'

'I see. I had no idea you were so well-qualified.'

Because he hadn't bothered to ask, she thought. No one at L'Alliance had made any effort to find out about her. Evidently they thought her only claim to her position was being Laurence Lowe's daughter.

It was unfair that they'd assumed she was unqualified, but she wouldn't push that point. She did wonder, though, whether the knowledge would make any difference to Pierre's review.

She'd planned for her position to be a passive one. She'd aimed to sit back and let Pierre do his review without trying to influence him, but also with no intention of agreeing to his recommendations. Perhaps she had taken the wrong path and should take a more active role in defending herself.

CHAPTER SIX

As THEY walked from the hotel to the restaurant, Pierre was glad to be out of the car, where Beth's perfume had nearly driven him crazy. Not that it was anything special—although he couldn't deny that as perfumes went its light floral tones were pleasant—but because it was hers. He'd have recognised it anywhere. It was irrevocably linked with her in the scent registry section of his brain. With her body, her skin...

Combined with the way she looked in her slinky dress, in the close confines of the car it had tortured him.

On the other hand, he'd delighted in their ability to have a non-confrontational conversation. Despite having been in different hemispheres for a decade, they still managed to have an incredible amount in common, it seemed. As long as they refrained from mentioning their past, and the purpose of his visit, it was almost as if they'd never been apart.

He smothered the wave of regret that surged through him. If she were any other woman he wouldn't hesitate to make a move. But there was no possibility of that, and no point in regretting it.

As soon as they walked through the door of the restaurant, Beth swung into action. She left him alone in the area set aside for pre-dinner drinks while she went to talk to the *maître d'*.

It was a little early for guests, and he had the space to himself. He sat on a padded bench running the length of one wall and observed her as she went about her business. There was no denying she looked beautiful in that dress. No, he corrected himself. She always looked beautiful. But the dress made her look…grown-up. Mature. He couldn't take his eyes off her. The perfect femininity of her. When she looked up and caught his eye, she gave him a little wave and a big smile. His gut contracted and he knew he'd lost the battle to be indifferent to her.

It had definitely been a mistake to come to Australia. For one evening, though, he wanted to forget the reason he was there. Forget the fact that Beth hated him and his job. Forget what had happened all those years ago. He wanted to experience the thrill of being near her again. Without barriers. Without pain.

Plenty of time to get back to business once they returned to the Barossa Valley. Until then, he'd relax and let the evening unfold—as he'd used to when he was young, when he hadn't felt the need to control everything around him.

The restaurant door opened and a group of guests entered. They nodded at him as they were shown into the drinks area, and almost immediately a waiter appeared with a tray of filled glasses. Chilled rosé, he announced. The bottle stood on the tray, and Pierre could see the Lowland label.

Within half an hour the small area was reverberating with anticipation of a pleasant evening. Pierre considered going in search of Beth, but the *maître d'* arrived at that moment to usher them into the main dining area.

Pierre found himself at the same table as Beth, but separated from her by an elderly couple. He did his best to hide his disappointment as he introduced himself to his immediate neighbours—silver-haired Alma on his right, and on his left an exotic-looking young woman with a mass of auburn-coloured curls. Tegan. As she spoke to Pierre, she leaned forward and touched his arm. He sighed silently and hoped Alma was the talkative type. He'd met plenty of Tegans and found them tiresome.

The *maître d'* strode into a space between the tables and welcomed the guests in a powerful voice more suited to the stage than the restaurant business. The man gestured at a display of the complete Lowland range, and then, with a glowing introduction, invited Beth to take the floor.

Pierre couldn't say what he'd expected, but Beth took his breath away with her confidence and poise—not to mention her beauty. And that smile. Glancing around the room, he could see guests, both male and female, becoming entranced as she spoke. Professional through and through, she described the wines they'd be served during the evening, and explained that she'd worked with the chef to ensure the food and wine would complement each other. She beamed around the room once again, and her sincerity shone through when she wished them all an enjoyable evening.

He gave her an approving nod as she moved back to

her seat, and when she grinned back he could have sworn his body temperature shot up a few degrees. Barely aware of the entrées being served, he tasted the Lowland Semillon as soon as the wine waiter poured it into his glass.

'I suppose, being French, you were weaned on wine?' Tegan said, leaning close.

'You could say that,' he answered, averting his eyes from the cleavage on display.

Relieved when one of the male guests across the table attracted Tegan's attention, he turned to speak to Alma. He made small talk with Alma and her husband until the time came for Beth to stand up again. This time she presented two red wines—a Shiraz and a Cabernet—to be served with the main course.

'Firstly, the 2002 Olive Branch Shiraz,' she said. 'It's an intense, yet supple wine, and though it's red it smells of guava, lychee and peach.'

She glanced around the room to confirm the wine waiters were making good progress, then invited her audience to sniff their glasses.

'Can you smell the very slight peppermint hints?' she asked. 'And there's a lovely light top note that smells like a bowl of ripe fruits soused in Kirsch.'

There was a low murmur of laughter at which Beth smiled. 'The palate is radically different from the 2001 vintage,' she went on. 'No porty overtones.'

She mesmerised him. Despite having spent his whole life around wine people, Pierre had never heard anyone put so much sensuality into a simple description. There was something about the sparkle in her eyes and her body language that said she revelled in sharing her product with people who appreciated it. He felt like a moth, drawn to the brightness of her.

'The aftertaste is bone-dry,' she said. 'I can't call to mind another wine of this strength that retains such fresh, svelte elegance and vibrant life.'

Fresh, svelte elegance and vibrant life described *her*, Pierre thought. Just as unique as her wine, there was simply no one else like her.

After Beth's introduction to the Cobby Creek Cabernet, she rejoined the table and immediately became absorbed in a lively conversation with the couple on her right. Pierre watched her with the growing realisation that he'd missed her. Missed everything about her. He had a hollow space inside him that she should have filled.

From time to time over the years friends had asked Pierre what kind of woman he was attracted to. Wanting to know what his type was. He'd never been able to answer them. But now, looking at Beth, he knew. *She* was his type. He couldn't name a category, because she was one of a kind. Like no other woman he'd ever known. Beth, and she alone, was his type.

Tegan squeezed his arm and flicked her abundant hair from her face. 'She's quite pretty, isn't she?' she asked, indicating Beth with a movement of her head.

Quite pretty?

Pierre jerked his arm away more roughly than he'd intended. He still hadn't come up with an appropriate response when one of the other diners tossed a question across the table at him, and for once he found himself grateful to enter into a comparison of government wine taxes.

After the main course, Beth pushed back her chair again. Time for her favourite part of the evening—when she could talk about anything she wanted, within reason.

'Generalising about vintage conditions in the Barossa Valley is as dangerous as saying all women drivers are bad,' she began, and was gratified at the laughter that rumbled around the room. It meant her audience was relaxed which was just how she wanted it. 'Neighbouring wineries will have a totally different experience of the same weather...'

She went on to talk about the latest vintage, and its effect on the most recent crop of Lowland wines, yet to be released. Next she drew a business card from a hat and announced the winner of a basket of Lowland products. And finally she asked the wine waiters to open a few bottles of the premium Century Hill, so guests could have a sample size taste of the sought-after Shiraz.

And then it was time for dessert. She returned to the table, pleased to see Pierre appeared comfortable. She hoped it was more to do with the conversation with the guy opposite than with the socialite sitting next to him. Or rather, almost sitting in his lap.

She pulled herself up. She wasn't his keeper. She wasn't anything to him. And besides, she couldn't blame the woman—he *was* the best-looking man in the room.

Ha! Who was she kidding? He was the best-looking man she'd ever seen. Ever.

'Beth?'

She jerked her eyes from Pierre as someone tapped her shoulder. She looked up at one of the guests from another table. She knew from an earlier dinner that he was a serious wine collector. 'Yes, Brendan?'

'I have to say it's rare to taste a suite of wines as accomplished and true to *terroir* as these.'

'Thank you, Brendan. I appreciate it. Coming from you, it's quite a compliment.'

'Not at all. I'm glad you've decided to limit production in order to maintain the quality of these wines. The worst thing you could do is import fruit from outside the region to boost output. I know others have done it, but Lowland is to be congratulated for not doing so.'

Beth felt Pierre's gaze on her, but resisted the urge to glance at him. 'I agree with you, Brendan. While I'm in charge, Lowland Wines will not change its philosophy.'

Brendan gasped. 'I know about the new majority shareholder, of course. But L'Alliance wouldn't risk Lowland's reputation, surely?'

With ears flapping around the room, she wished she'd been more careful in her choice of words. She took a sip of the sticky Muscat served to accompany dessert. 'Just a figure of speech, Brendan. I didn't mean anything by it.'

Brendan gave her a serious look and lowered his voice. 'They wouldn't kick you out, Beth. They'd be crazy to do so.'

'Brendan, please don't worry. I'm not going anywhere.' She gave him her best smile and he left—mollified, she hoped.

As she turned back to the table, with the tail-end of the smile still in place, she met Pierre's gaze before his attention was reclaimed by the redhead. Beth lifted her chin. She refused to believe the sudden ache in her chest was jealousy, but it felt suspiciously like it.

Pierre's eyes widened as Tegan whispered in his ear. Beth didn't want to think about what she might have said. She looked away in disgust, pleased the *maître d'* chose that moment to appear at her shoulder to let her know that they were about to serve the coffee.

Mingling and chatting, Beth lost sight of Pierre. But eventually the last of the guests took their leave and they were the only two in the room besides the restaurant employees. She was shocked at the relief she felt when she saw Tegan had left. Shocked at how anxious she'd been that he might go home with Tegan.

She crossed the room to him. 'Did you have a good time?'

'I had an excellent time, thank you. You were magnificent.'

'Magnificent?' She laughed. 'Steady on. That's over the top.'

'Not at all. Everyone said so.'

She narrowed her eyes at him and he shrugged.

'Only a slight exaggeration. Are you ready to go?'

She nodded, and as they made their way out, with a wave to the staff, he took her hand. It felt natural. Strange, after so long, but natural.

By the time they reached the hotel Beth was desperate to bank down the fire that had burst into life. It was ridiculous. How could she be so attracted to him in spite of everything?

She didn't know how, but 'attracted' didn't begin to cover what she felt. Not nearly.

As they approached the main entrance, she felt reluctant to end such a lovely evening. Ever since they'd left the winery that afternoon it had been almost like old times. She'd made an effort, and Pierre had seemed to make a similar effort. It seemed they'd done a good job of convincing themselves there was no problem. Maybe too good.

'It's a pleasant night,' Pierre said. 'It seems a pity to go inside. Would you like to take a walk?'

'Yes, I'd like that.' She shivered.

'Cold? Perhaps we'd better go inside?'

'No, not cold. It was just a breeze from the river.' And thoughts she couldn't admit to.

On a high from the success of the dinner, she looked up at the massed fairy lights in the trees and sighed. 'This is nice, isn't it?'

'Yes.' After a moment, he said, 'The lights are nice too.'

They turned at the corner and strolled until they reached the road bridge over the Torrens River. There they stopped to watch the illuminated fountain shoot sparkling drops of water into the night sky.

A few minutes passed, then Beth became aware of being the only one watching the fountain. Pierre was watching her. And the way he looked at her took her by surprise. Like a starving man studying a loaf of bread.

Goosebumps prickled her bare arms, and she couldn't tell whether they came from the cool night air or awareness of that look. She recognised it. It meant he wanted to kiss her. She felt queasy.

He turned his back on the fountain and leaned against the stone bridge wall. Close to her. Very close. She shivered again, and he rubbed her bare arms in a tender gesture. The light friction warmed her skin and turned up the temperature inside her.

His fingers stilled and tightened on her arms. Then he drew her towards him till there was no more space between them. With a tiny moan of anticipation, she closed her eyes and gave in to the moment. She didn't think about the past, and certainly not the future. She concentrated on the sensation of being back in Pierre's arms, absorbing the heat from his body, and lifted her lips for his kiss.

His mouth, hesitant at first, touched hers as if he couldn't quite believe he was kissing her. Sweet and gentle. Then a little firmer, more urgent. In response, she felt something stir in her stomach. A pulsing, throbbing and long-suppressed need that took her breath away.

She moaned again, and he broke the kiss to look at her face, but then he was back and kissing her deeply, with an intimacy that startled her with its novelty and frightened her with its familiarity. Exciting, yet comforting. Exhilarating, yet like coming home.

He opened her lips with the firm pressure of his tongue and explored her mouth. She met him there, and their tongues slid against each other, making her thighs tingle.

He crushed her to him, and the sensation of her breasts against his chest, with only the thin, silky fabric of her dress between them, made her throb. She slid her own hands inside his jacket, flattening her fingers against the firm muscles of his back.

She wanted to stay like that, as close as she could get to him. Kissing and being kissed. Tasting and being tasted. Loving and—

The realisation hit her like a tidal wave. In the face of its power she had no choice but to admit she loved him. Loved, wanted, needed. It scared her to death.

She tensed, and doing so allowed the truth of their situation to flood back into her consciousness. She broke away, twisting out of his arms to clutch the bridge parapet, desperate for its solidity.

How could she have been so stupid? She'd behaved like an idiot. Worse. Intoxicated. Not by wine, but by the sexual tension that had existed between them from the moment they'd left the restaurant. So much for being professional. She was angry with herself. So angry.

'We shouldn't have done that,' she said, her voice shaky but more controlled than she'd expected.

She tried to focus on him standing there, fists clenched at his sides, his face bleak.

'It wasn't... I mean...' She pushed both hands through her hair, not caring how it looked. 'I didn't want to do that,' she stated flatly. 'I seriously did *not* want to kiss you.'

He stared back at her without a word, but she knew he'd heard by the tightening of his jaw. The words *Who are you kidding?* hung between them, though neither of them spoke. Tears sprang to her eyes, and she wiped them away with the back of her hand.

Beth swung around and headed back to the hotel as fast as she could walk. Her breath came in short rasps from deep inside. When she reached her room, she closed the door behind her and allowed the tears to flow.

And flow they did. They were tears that had been bottled up for too long. She'd allowed emotion to surface when she'd kissed Pierre, and in so doing had unlocked the lid keeping her pain hidden and under control. Now she'd let it out, and it wouldn't be pushed away again until she acknowledged it.

So she wept for her shattered illusions of love all those years before. For ten years she'd denied herself the healing process of grieving. When she'd returned home she hadn't told anyone about her pain. She'd hidden it, and hoped ignoring it would make it go away.

And she cried for her father—for the time she hadn't spent with him and all the ways she'd let him down. She mourned her loss for the first time. The loss of a father to turn to for support, to learn from. The loss of her family.

Until that point her burden of guilt, remorse for what she hadn't done, had prevented her from grieving and accepting her own loss.

And finally she sobbed for the man she'd left on the bridge. She couldn't deny the truth. Despite what he'd done to her in the past, despite what he was going to do to her winery, she loved Pierre still. In the present.

Yet there was no future for them. That kiss hadn't been the start of something new between them. It had been an echo of the past. He hadn't come to Australia to regain what he'd lost. He was here for another reason entirely. And it was that that stopped her in her tracks.

She'd been so close to giving in to her physical need for him. Thank God she'd come to her senses. He'd be in the country for a short time, then he'd be gone. Taking with him her winery *and* the fragile remains of her heart.

Beth's tears stopped flowing as she sat, frozen, contemplating the awful possibility that the kiss had been planned. A deliberate ploy to soften her up. To make her more amenable to his proposals for the winery.

Perhaps that was why he'd been chosen to come to the Barossa? Not a coincidence, but a carefully considered strategy for L'Alliance to gain the upper hand. Because he knew her weakness. Because he *was* her weakness....

CHAPTER SEVEN

PIERRE thrust his hands into his pockets and started back to the hotel. She'd rejected him again. Would he never learn?

He'd gone into that kiss with his eyes wide open. A little clouded, granted, by the effects of such a pleasant evening, but he'd known what he was doing. And he should have known better.

So why had he done it? Why had he kissed her? Because she'd looked extraordinary? Because she was a fascinating mixture of vulnerability and competence? Because, as soon as he'd touched her, all semblance of logic had slipped away and he'd been overwhelmed by memories of the incredible lovemaking they'd once shared?

She'd tasted so sweet—of wine, of dessert—and also just as he remembered her tasting. He'd kissed her as if he'd forgotten everything but the fact that he was with her, the woman he'd never been able to get out of his head…or his heart.

And for a long moment there he'd believed she felt the same way. That she had the same need to revisit the passion they'd known. The way she'd melted against him, into him, as if she'd been waiting for him. The way her lips, her mouth, had welcomed his. No restraint. No doubts. Right up until she'd wrenched herself out of his arms.

He'd learned his lesson at last. He wouldn't be tempted again. His future wasn't here. It was in France. With Philippe. That was what was important. More than ever he wanted to finish his report and fly out. He would fulfil his duties as a director of Lowland Wines from overseas, and only return when he absolutely had to.

The next morning, Beth peered through her fingers at the mirror, not wanting to risk a full-frontal stare at her sleep-deprived and tear-ravaged face. What a mess! And not just her face.

Pity they hadn't travelled separately. Then they wouldn't have to endure the long drive back to the Barossa together. As it was, she couldn't even lick her wounds in private.

She dressed in the jeans and shirt she'd brought with her, and drank some black tea, but winced at the aroma of toast on the room service tray. She'd filled in the order before dinner. She'd had no idea then that her stomach would be awash with swirling emotions. Until she got it under control, eating seemed like a bad idea.

With a final frank glance in the mirror at her red-rimmed, puffy eyes, she picked up her overnight bag and left the room. On her way down in the lift she wondered how Pierre would react when they met. A current of apprehension coursed through her. But she had her guard up now, and there would be no more tears. She'd cried herself empty.

The lift doors opened, and she saw Pierre in a plush armchair in the foyer, reading a newspaper. As she walked up to him she recognised it was the French paper *Le Monde*. He must have been out early to buy it from the city railway station.

He didn't seem to notice her—or if he did he made no move to greet her. The stark expression on his face when he did eventually turn his head sent Beth's stomach into a slow roll, and she was thankful she hadn't eaten breakfast. She didn't need to deal with his anger on top of everything else she felt. She would only manage to muddle through if they both remained polite. *She* intended to behave as if nothing had happened.

'Have you been waiting long?' she asked.

'Half an hour or so.'

She nodded. 'Shall we go?'

He folded his newspaper, tucked it under his arm, picked up his garment bag from beside the chair and headed for the main door. All without looking at her.

As she followed him, Beth saw at least two women glance his way, their eyes lingering. She didn't blame them. Whether dressed up in a suit or down in jeans, as he was now, he was striking. Quite apart from looks, he had something else…a presence. Charisma. Maybe that was the word for it. Whatever, he turned heads. And he'd had her head in a spin the evening before, but not now. She had control of herself again. All her feelings were safely tucked back in their box. She was wise to his scheme and she would not be sucked into it.

'Can I have my keys, please?' Beth asked as they reached the car.

He pulled them out of his pocket, but held on to them for a moment. 'I don't mind driving,' he said, still not meeting her gaze.

'No, thank you. I will.' She wanted to drive. It would keep her mind occupied.

He shrugged, handed over the keys, and climbed into the passenger seat. Once seated, she made three attempts to tug her seatbelt out before taking a deep breath and making a conscious effort to slide it smoothly from its housing.

She started the engine.

'About last night on the bridge,' he said. 'I'd like to apologise. It was—*I* was unprofessional.'

She shook her head. 'Let's not discuss it. I'd prefer to forget it ever happened.'

'I agree.'

'Fine, then.'

'Fine.'

She pulled out into the traffic and Pierre slumped further down in his seat. She hoped he intended to sleep, because small-talk would be difficult for both of them in the circumstances.

Pierre opened his eyes the instant she parked the car outside her house, making her suspect he'd only pretended to sleep. He got out and waited for her to unlock the boot.

'Hi, there, how did it go?' Tasha called. She strode towards them as Beth stepped out of the car.

'Fine, thanks, Tash. Migraine all gone?'

'Yup. What did you think of it?' she asked Pierre, hooking an arm through his and smiling up at him.

'The dinner was very good,' he said, shifting his weight, looking uncomfortable.

Beth could see he didn't welcome Tasha's attention. Tough, she thought, because she certainly didn't intend to help him.

Tasha wanted him to elaborate. 'Very good? Is that all? Didn't you think our Beth was wonderful?'

He made a non-committal noise.

Magnificent, he'd said. But maybe that had been a calculated part of the build-up to his planned kiss. Well, she wasn't a girl any more, to be taken in by his compliments and kisses. His scheme had backfired. She was a grown woman, with a winery to save, and she was not about to allow her personal loneliness to lead her into breaking a deathbed promise to her father.

Beth opened the boot of the car and removed her bag, then waited for Pierre to extricate himself from Tasha and collect his garment bag.

'I left my laptop in your office yesterday,' he said. 'I would like to work in there for a while, if you don't mind?'

'Right. I have some urgent work to do too. I'll unpack, then head over to unlock the office.'

When Beth came out of the house a few minutes later, she found Tasha leaning against the car, waiting for her.

'What have you done to Pierre?' She pushed off the vehicle and fell in alongside Beth as she walked towards the office.

'Why? Did he say something?' A spark of anger made Beth's tone sharp.

Tasha gave her a curious look. 'No. But there's something wrong. I've got frostbite from standing between you.'

'Of course not. We're both tired, that's all.'

Tasha snorted. 'All right, so you don't want to tell me what's going on. I thought I was your friend.' She shrugged.

Beth's insides twisted. 'You are. You're my best friend, Tash. It's just…Pierre and I disagree on some aspects of winery management.' She sighed. 'Don't worry. We'll work it out.' *As if.* They were diametrically opposed. There was no way they'd be able to meet in the middle.

'Hmm. Okay. I thought I'd ask him to dinner at my place tonight. Is it all right with you?'

'Why shouldn't it be?'

'Well, I wondered whether something had happened…after the dinner…at the hotel?'

He was already at the office door.

'Shh. No. *No*—definitely not.'

Beth moved ahead of Tasha to unlock it, remembering she'd meant to oil the hinges as it creaked open. She wouldn't tell Tasha what had happened between them. No matter how much she probed. Beth avoided eye contact with Pierre as she entered the room.

'I'm here to deliver a personal invitation,' Tasha said in a bright voice. 'To dinner, tonight, at my house.'

'Ah. I don't think…'

From the corner of her eye Beth saw him glance her way, but she kept her eyes fixed on Tasha. He appeared to flounder, searching for an excuse.

'Well…'

'Good. I'll take that as a yes,' Tasha said. 'It'll be fun. I'll let you know when I close up the cellar door, and you can come home with me.'

He nodded, a resigned expression on his face. 'Thank you.'

It occurred to Beth that she could have enlisted Tasha to persuade Pierre into seeing things her way. Tasha would have been only too willing to play the *femme fatale*. But, no. *He* might work that way. *She* didn't. She hit the button to switch on her computer. The angry action made him look her way, but she ignored him, sat down and dragged the keyboard close.

As they planned to use the screw-top Stelvin caps that year, they needed a new range of bottles to suit them. The bottle manufacturers had promised to e-mail her the necessary information so she could place an order, and she couldn't afford to delay making a decision or the bottles wouldn't be here on time. As much as she would have liked to leave Pierre alone, her work was just as important as his. Even if she wouldn't be there to see the vintage bottled, it would go ahead. It had to. Too many livelihoods depended on it.

After working in silence for nearly an hour, Pierre cleared his throat, then asked her for information on yields from the various vineyards.

'How far back do you want to go?' She chewed her bottom lip. Those were the only records she hadn't transferred to the computer, and they dated from her father's purchase of the property.

'I'm only interested in current data, and the figures from the last few years for comparison purposes,' he said.

With her back to him, she retrieved the necessary files from the cabinets lining one wall. It had been a strain to sit so close to him without speaking, but she knew it was safer to stick to essential conversation only.

She spread the files on the desk. 'Where do you want to start? Which wine?'

He shrugged. 'Anywhere.'

She flipped open the first file. 'Okay—Shiraz. Century Hill yield last year was one and a half tonnes per acre—'

'That's very low.'

She looked up, connecting with his intense gaze and wishing she hadn't. 'Yes, but remember this is our premium wine. The vines are dry-grown, to ensure maximum concentration of flavours.'

He looked thoughtful for a moment, then typed something into his laptop. 'Go on.'

She rattled off the yields for all the wines, then sat back and watched him type. Concentrating, he looked less like a ruthless executive and more like the young man he'd been. She dug her nails into her palms. She had to stop thinking that way. She had to stay in the present.

'Beth. Are you okay?'

She blinked once, twice. There in front of her Pierre the business man sat, scrutinising her. Big mistake to let her thoughts wander.

'Are you all right?'

What a ridiculous question. She'd been torn apart and stuck back together, but the pieces didn't quite fit. She sucked in a deep breath. 'Yes, of course I'm all right. Why wouldn't I be?'

He stared at her. 'You didn't hear me. I asked a question. Several times.'

'Did you? Sorry, I was miles away.' She took another deep, steadying breath. 'What did you want to know?'

He stared a moment longer. 'About water. How you manage it.'

'Water. Yes. Right. With the exception of the dry-grown Shiraz vines, we monitor moisture using a neutron probe at various depths throughout the vine-yards. The readings govern the amount of water that is applied via a computerised drip irrigation system. Recently we—that is, the region's growers—paid for the construction of a pipeline to bring water from the Murray River. It will mean consistent water quality and assure a ready supply for the dry years. Is that what you wanted to know?'

He nodded, and gathered his notes together before shutting down the laptop. 'I'll work at The Barn for the rest of the day,' he said.

'I'll let Tasha know where to find you.'

'Thank you.' He didn't look up. 'Tomorrow, I'd like to talk to you about the changes I will recommend to the Board.'

Beth stiffened. 'You've finished your review?'

He glanced up, but she didn't have an opportunity to read his expression before he looked away again. 'Yes, I've finished. You'll be pleased to know I'll be leaving soon.'

CHAPTER EIGHT

PIERRE shuffled from foot to foot and swapped his laptop case from one hand to the other as he waited outside Beth's locked office. He wanted to get their meeting over and done with. Why wasn't she here? What did she think she'd gain by delaying it?

He'd covered all the cost comparisons, plotted all the graphs and examined all the options. Now all he had to do was convince her.

Correction: he didn't have to convince her. There was no obligation for him to show her the right way to go about business, to give her an opportunity to safeguard her position. Yet for some inexplicable reason he wanted to make her understand. He hoped to spare her the humiliation of losing control of her winery. For old times' sake—not because he still cared. He didn't. She'd walked all over his feelings for the last time.

If he could persuade her to take one or other of the directions he'd outlined, she'd be able to stay on. Though she'd have to fall in line with the dictates of L'Alliance management, she'd still make the day-to-day decisions. She *had* to see the sense in that.

He glanced at his watch. Was she avoiding him? He'd be surprised if she took a coward's way out. Maybe she had a problem at the house? Maybe she was ill? She had looked as if she was in pain the previous day. Perhaps he should check.

Just then he saw her car heading along the driveway. She'd been out early. He let out a sigh of relief, glad he'd be able to go ahead with his explanations. He hadn't wanted to bypass her and go straight to the Board.

She parked the car in front of the office and hopped out, turning towards him with a radiant smile. It faltered slightly as they made eye contact, and lost some of its warmth. Wherever she'd been it had made her happy, and the logical deduction hit him like a right hook to the chin. Had she spent the night with a man?

He made a conscious effort to unclench his jaw before entering the office behind her.

'Sorry I'm late,' she said over her shoulder. 'It was an incredible night.'

He balled his fists as he waited for the computer to start up. He'd got the message loud and clear. She could spare him the details. He shook his head, ignoring her questioning glance as she removed her jacket. She shrugged out of it and a teasing glimpse of tanned, taut midriff appeared below a skin-tight T-shirt. A swirly skirt clung to her hips and stopped short of her knees. Together, the clothes did nothing to hide her figure and everything to disrupt his train of thought.

She broke into a smile again as she sat down. Then the door creaked open and he groaned inwardly as he saw Tasha enter. It had been a most embarrassing evening at Tasha's house. Twice in two days he'd had to reject a blatant proposition from a woman. First Tegan, then Tasha. Both beautiful women in their own right, but they did nothing for him. How could they? But maybe it was time he made an effort to find another woman attractive. He had to get Beth out of his system once and for all.

Tasha nodded in his direction, then sat in a chair facing Beth.

'So, it's finally happened?'

'Yes.' Beth nodded, grinning. 'During the night.' She hugged herself. 'It was a wonderful experience.'

He looked from one woman to the other. He knew Australians were broad-minded as a nation, but this was ridiculous. He coughed, to remind them of his presence. They both glanced across, but when he didn't speak they returned to their conversation.

'Congratulations!' Tasha said. 'And? Give me details.'

Pierre sank lower in the chair. *Unbelievable.* He should walk out.

'A girl. She has masses of spiky black hair, and her skin's a lovely creamy colour—not all blotchy like a lot of newborn babies.'

A baby? He frowned as he erased his assumption and replaced it with this new information.

'Name? Weight? Come on, Beth.'

'Sorry. I'm still totally overawed by the whole thing. They're going to call her Laura Elizabeth. Laura is for Laurence—after my dad, of course. And Elizabeth is—well, after me. Isn't that sweet of them?'

Tasha nodded. 'Understandable, though. You two are like saints to the Himmels.'

Beth made a dismissive gesture, then leaned back in her chair, stretching her arms above her head. 'I'm so tired.'

Pierre dragged his eyes away. He wished he was impervious to her, just as she was to him.

'So, when does your goddaughter come home?' Tasha asked.

'Goddaughter?'

The two women turned to look at him.

'You have a goddaughter?'

'I do now. She was born last night, and I was there for the birth.' Beth turned back to Tasha. 'Corinne and Laura should be discharged from Tanunda Hospital later today. They're both fine, so I don't expect they'll have to stay in longer.'

'I'll wait till they're home before I visit,' Tasha said. She pushed back the chair and stood up. 'I'd better go open up the cellar door.'

Once Tasha had left, Pierre looked at Beth's faraway expression. Time to bring her back to earth. 'When will you be ready for me to outline the options?' he asked.

'I'll be with you in a moment,' she said. 'I just want to check my e-mail.'

Pierre watched her. After a few mouse-clicks, she grinned broadly at the screen in front of her.

'Karl Himmel has sent me some photos from his digital camera,' she said. 'He promised he would.' She swivelled the monitor to face him. 'Here's Laura Elizabeth,' she said with pride.

Pierre looked at the screen. He couldn't make out

much of the baby wrapped tightly in a blanket. All he could see was her nose. Beth clicked the mouse.

'Here's another one,' she said. 'It's a bit clearer.'

This time it was Beth on the screen, and he drew in a sharp breath. She sat on the edge of a hospital bed, cradling the baby in her arms and smiling into the camera. The picture made something in his chest twist and crack. This was how Beth would have looked holding *their* child. As she should have done. As he'd wanted her to.

'Isn't she gorgeous?'

He nodded, finding speech impossible at that moment. Beth swung the screen away.

He swore silently, and rubbed his forehead with a thumb and forefinger. He had a headache. Not to mention a constant ache in his chest. It felt like indigestion, but he knew it couldn't be. He'd never suffered from a poor digestive system before he came to Australia. He had to finish the job he'd been sent to do and get out of the country as quickly as possible, before he became a physical wreck.

'Let's get down to business,' he said, sounding more brusque than he'd meant to.

Her face fell as suddenly as if he'd reached across the desk and swiped the smile from it. She nodded. 'Fine.'

He strode to the whiteboard on the wall and, picking up one of the felt-tipped pens from the ledge beneath it, began to write in large, bold letters.

'Your goal,' he said as he finished writing and capped the pen, 'must be to increase production in order to increase turnover and therefore profit. L'Alliance management is happy with your present profit margin. However, the total on which that margin is calculated is too small.'

'Why?'

He glanced at Beth, with her arms folded defensively across her chest.

'Because L'Alliance says it is. In comparison with other companies of the same type and size, both in Australia and in other parts of the world, Lowland's contribution to corporate profit is low. You have three options,' he said.

Beth looked as if she wanted to shoot him. And he couldn't blame her. He wasn't just the messenger, he was the author. But he would make the recommendation whether it meant she stayed or went. He turned his back on her and underlined the first two words, giving himself a moment to steel himself.

'Option one,' he said, 'is to increase production by purchasing larger quantities of raw materials. Costs, however, could be kept relatively static by buying more cheaply. I have prepared a cost comparison chart.'

He crossed to his laptop, brought up a file on the screen, and pushed it across the desk towards Beth.

She sat forward to peer at the screen. 'By raw materials, I assume you mean the grapes? The very heart and soul of the wine?'

'Yes,' he said simply. He had to keep to the facts. He did not want to get into an argument with Beth. This was too important. 'From my chart you can see how much more fruit you'd be able to buy if you imported it from interstate, or even overseas.'

'Never.'

'Please look at the figures. This is not the time for emotion. Consider the facts. They speak for themselves.'

She pursed her lips and slumped back in the chair.

He stifled a sigh and returned to the whiteboard. 'Option two,' he said, 'is to increase the quantity of grapes you purchase locally.'

She looked up, her eyes narrowed.

'To do this, however, you would have to negotiate more favourable terms with your growers. If they want the business, they'll play ball. If not—' he shrugged '—there are other growers.'

Beth snorted. 'If you think I'd do that—' She glared at him, and he felt the daggers from her eyes. He took a steadying breath.

'Then we have option three. You could increase output by employing better vineyard management methods.'

'Excuse me?' She sounded incredulous.

He turned to avoid seeing the outrage in her face. After pretending to read the bullet points on the whiteboard for a moment, he faced her again.

'You could increase yields, particularly of Shiraz, by introducing water to the dry vineyards.'

'You're kidding? Why would we want to do that?'

'As I said—to increase yields and therefore output.'

'And ruin our premium wine? The Century Hill? It's the dry-farmed vineyard that produces the rich aroma and weighty structure.'

'You'd have more to sell.'

She stared at him, and he picked up the whiteboard eraser, tapping it against his leg, waiting for her reaction. When it came, her tone was flat, her anger under control.

'I can't believe you said that, Pierre. You must know what a ridiculous suggestion it is. And you know I can't possibly agree to it.'

He used the whiteboard eraser to wipe the surface of the board with long, slow strokes. 'I'm doing my job,' he said, without looking at her.

'Well, your job stinks.'

He flinched. 'You have until tomorrow's Board Meeting to decide which option you prefer. If you choose to resist all three, I will recommend a change in managing director.'

He replaced the eraser and turned to see a flush spreading over Beth's cheeks.

'I can tell you now,' she said. 'I have no intention of taking up any of those options.'

'In that case, I wish you luck in your search for another position.' His heart beat hard in his chest—like it did after his morning run, but without the pleasant buzz.

'Don't think I'll give in so easily,' she said with surprising firmness. 'I'll present my case to the Board. I'll ask them to support me.'

He looked at her without speaking. They'd chew her up and spit her out. She didn't stand a chance.

The next morning, Beth dressed carefully for the Board Meeting in a tailored black skirt and cream linen blouse. Her hands shook as she poked the tiny cream buttons into their holes.

She'd told Pierre she would ask the directors to

support her. If only she could be sure they would. They knew how hard she'd worked. They knew how much the winery meant to her. And they knew her father had asked her, immediately before his death to continue his life's work. They knew all this. Yet none of it had stopped them voting in favour of the takeover.

She'd tried her best to talk them out of it, to make them see something other than dollar signs. But only her cousin Simon had voted with her. So why did she think she could make a difference now?

She grimaced at her reflection. She didn't know whether she could or not, but whatever happened she had to try. She owed it to her father to put up a fight against L'Alliance, and she had no intention of letting him down again. She had to remain calm, keep her cool, maintain her dignity. She'd gain nothing but pity if she broke down. She couldn't allow that to happen. She couldn't let the directors see tears. Especially Pierre.

A lump rose to her throat and she swallowed slowly, repeatedly, determined to take control of her emotions. When she stood to speak, she had to make it clear that she was not there to be a push-over. That she was not about to roll over and play dead so Pierre and his boss could have their way.

Pierre had tried to tell her their way was best. He'd attempted to talk her round, to convince her that her father's principles weren't worth fighting for. Weren't worth losing her job over. Her skin grew hot at the thought of his kiss. How far would he have gone if she hadn't made it clear she couldn't be swayed?

And what would have happened if she hadn't recognised the kiss for the manipulation it was? What would have happened if she'd allowed herself to trust him?

He'd have dumped her and left. Of that she had no doubt.

She squeezed her eyes shut. Anyway, he was wrong. Principles were everything.

Profit was important, of course. Without it the winery would go under. Like his father's. She could see such an experience colouring his thinking. He'd loved that winery.

But profit wasn't everything. Whole families depended on this business. Not only those of her direct employees, but those of the growers whose vineyards were their livelihood. Their life. She refused to even consider selling them out. It would be a monstrous betrayal. Of them. Of her father.

If she lost today, if the directors still voted against her after her presentation, at least she'd have the satisfaction of knowing she'd put everything she had into doing the right thing. It would still be devastating, but it wouldn't be because she hadn't tried.

'Coo-eee.'

Beth's eyes flew open at the sound of Tasha's call. 'In here,' she called.

The bedroom door opened and Tasha poked her head around it. 'I wondered if you could buy something for me while you're in Adelaide? Some of those cute baby clothes for Laura Elizabeth?'

'What?' Beth stared at her friend for a moment. Baby clothes were the furthest thing from her mind this morning. 'Oh, yes,' she said vaguely. 'I will if I have the time.' She took her short black jacket from its hanger and slipped it on.

Tasha watched her in the mirror as she straightened the jacket's lapels.

'It's only a Board Meeting, Beth.'

'I know, I know.' She couldn't tell Tasha it was the most important meeting of her life.

'So why have you bitten your fingernails right down? I thought you kicked that habit years ago.'

Beth looked at the damage she'd done. 'Damn. What a mess.'

'Are you going to tell me what's going on?'

'There's nothing going on.'

'Why are you nervous about this Board Meeting? You've been to plenty before. They've never affected you like this.'

'I'm not nervous.' She avoided Tasha's gaze as she bent to retrieve her shoes from the bottom of the wardrobe. 'Pierre's going to be there. We're going to thrash out a few things. That's all. No big deal.'

'Is he going to talk about his review?'

'Um...I expect so.' She glanced at her watch. 'I have to go now.'

Tasha held out some money. 'This should be enough for the baby clothes. And don't worry about Pierre's review,' she said as they headed to the front door. 'It'll be fine. It's just routine. What could he possibly have found to criticise?'

Beth held her breath as she looked around the Boardroom table, listening to the initial reactions of the directors to Pierre's presentation. She had to admit it had been very impressive. *He'd* been very impressive. She couldn't blame them for the positive vibes.

Now it was up to her to turn them around. No point in delaying. She pushed back her chair and made her way to the space he'd vacated. A slight trace of his classy aftershave hung in the air and mingled with the aroma of percolating coffee. She closed her mind to the memories the scents triggered. She had to concentrate.

With her back to the room, Beth opened the presentation on her laptop. She'd been up most of the night preparing it, and she knew that in design and professional polish it would more than equal what Pierre had shown the directors. But it was the content that was vital. Had she done a good enough job?

Despite her pounding pulse, she was ready. She sent up a silent prayer for her father's help and felt a cloak of composure settle around her. She fixed a smile on her face, and turned to face her audience.

'Thank you, Pierre, for your presentation. I'm sure everyone was impressed by your knowledge of the international wine market.' She waited for the murmur to die down. 'When it comes to Lowland Wines, however, I'm afraid you've got it wrong. Very wrong.'

She didn't allow her gaze to linger on his face. 'I know you've all seen my business plan before, but I've taken the liberty of printing off another copy for each of you.' She reached forward to place the documents in the centre of the table. 'Because it seems some of it, if not all of it, has been overlooked by L'Alliance management.'

She smiled. No time to indulge in anger that her own views had been ignored. She moved to her laptop and switched the presentation to the large screen, clicking to bring up the first slide.

'According to what we've heard from Pierre, there is only one way to increase profit—and that is by stepping up production. Granted, he presented us with three options, but all three are based on increasing output.' Beth made eye contact in turn with each of the directors. With the exception of one. 'Gentlemen, I intend to show you how an equivalent increase in profit can be achieved without destroying everything Lowland Wines stands for.'

After allowing a moment for her words to sink in, Beth turned to the screen.

'Here are the proposed profit figures based on Pierre's options one, two and three.'

Clicking the mouse button, she brought up one more figure to sit alongside the others.

'And here is the predicted increase in profit based on the proposals in my existing business plan.'

There was an astonished gasp from at least one of the directors. Beth shot a questioning look around the table. 'I gather some of you are surprised to see that I was already forecasting an upturn in profit without any proposed increase in production?'

She intercepted a grin from Simon, and struggled for a moment to keep her own face straight.

Brian King, in his seat at the head of the table, cleared his throat. 'I admit it's been a while since I've read your business plan, Beth. Can you remind us how you propose to achieve this upturn?'

'Of course, Brian. It would be my pleasure.' She hid her smile and clicked to the next slide.

CHAPTER NINE

BETH had removed her jacket and undone the top two buttons of her blouse, but she still felt hot. In the empty Boardroom she stood beneath the air-conditioning vent and lifted her hair from her neck, in the hope of catching even the slightest stream of cool air. Giving up, she began to pack away her laptop.

'We need to talk.'

Startled, she looked up and saw Pierre standing in the doorway. Somehow he managed to look immaculate, despite the heat. She clicked her tongue in exasperation.

'That's what the Board expects us to do,' she said, as she disconnected her computer from the projector and tucked the cable into the case.

'Yes, it is.' He closed the door and walked further into the room.

She glanced up. 'Could you open the door? It's hot in here. I think there's something wrong with the air-conditioning.'

'In a moment.' He gripped the back of one of the tall leather chairs ranged around the table. 'I think I owe you an apology,' he said.

She paused in the act of zipping up, and gave him a questioning look.

'In fact, I know I do.'

A range of emotions rattled through her, and she steadied herself against the table before she spoke. 'For what, exactly?'

'I underestimated you, and I'm sorry.'

She lifted her chin. 'Sorry the decision didn't go your way?'

He flinched, but stood his ground. 'I'm trying to apologise. Obviously I'm not very good at it. Perhaps my command of the English language is not as good as I thought.'

She rolled her eyes. 'Your English is perfect and you know it. What exactly are you trying to apologise for?'

He hesitated. 'For treating you as if you didn't understand the wine business.'

She tilted her head to one side and narrowed her eyes.

'You gave a first-class presentation,' he said.

'That's kind of patronising, Pierre. Why wouldn't I?'

He held out his palms. 'I'm sorry. I can't say the right thing, can I?'

Twitching her eyebrows, she returned to her packing. 'So, what was first-class? Are you talking about the delivery or the content?'

'Both.'

Their gazes locked for a moment, then with one hand she swung the laptop bag onto her shoulder. 'Well, thank you.'

'Why didn't you tell me about your plans for converting the old buildings, and all the other projects you have underway?'

With her other hand, she lifted the briefcase. 'Why didn't you read my business plan?'

'*Touché.*'

Walking to the window, he pushed his hands into his pockets, leaned one shoulder against the frame and stared down at the city's central business district.

'I was only interested in the current and historical figures. I didn't give you credit for having considered the future development of the business. I feel slightly foolish.'

'Only slightly?' She smiled. 'Neither you nor Frank gave me any credit at all.' She shrugged. 'Not that you were the only ones.'

'Excuse me?'

She shook her head. 'It's nothing.'

His gaze was intense. 'You have the directors' support.'

She jerked her head. 'So they say. Even so, they haven't given it completely, have they?'

'No, but a certain amount of caution…' He shrugged.

The Board had delayed the vote after hearing her presentation. They seemed inclined to support her. They professed to be on her side. However, they'd asked Pierre to examine her proposals and report on the accuracy of her predictions.

It was a slap in the face, showing they didn't trust her qualifications and experience, but it was one she could get over. She knew she'd done the research to back up her assumptions. And she could understand their reluctance to put their own fortunes in her hands without double-checking her proposals.

After staring at him in silence for a moment, Beth placed her bags on the table and slid into the nearest chair, leaning her elbows on the mahogany surface.

'Dad was a legend. Everyone in the valley respected him. Make that everyone in the Australian wine industry. He had an aura about him. People listened to him. His opinions mattered. And when he died…'

She turned her hands palm up and stared at them for a moment. 'Well, suddenly there was just little old me. How could I possibly take his place?'

Looking up as Pierre sat opposite her, she blinked back tears. No crying in front of him.

'Go on,' he said.

She lifted one shoulder in a half-hearted shrug. 'There's not much more to say. The Board had been used to Laurence Lowe, Barossa Valley icon, now they were reduced to dealing with his daughter, who'd only been in the industry for five minutes. They felt short-changed, naturally. Since I took over it's been one long battle to gain their respect. If I'd had their full support they would never have voted in favour of accepting the L'Alliance takeover bid.'

'But from what I've seen today you are one very capable woman.'

She gave a snort. 'Like that makes a difference.'

'I know I haven't been receptive to your opinions, Beth, but things will be different from now on. *I* will be different.'

She lifted her chin. 'I don't understand. Are you saying you're going to help me?'

'It seems to me the Board wants you to prove you are

your father's daughter.' He leaned forward and fixed her with his dark stare. 'As I see it, this is your opportunity to show them he was right to want you to take over from him.'

Her chest tightened. What was he doing? She didn't know if she could cope with him being kind to her. She'd just learned to deal with his opposition. She stared at the tabletop.

'We need to work together,' he said. 'If you're going to do that.'

He was right. She had to take advantage of her stronger position and his willingness to listen. She dragged in a breath and nodded at him.

'Yes, I agree. But now…' She glanced at her watch. 'Now, I have to go shopping. I'll meet you at the car in, say, one hour?'

He pushed back the chair and stood. 'I'll come with you.'

She laughed. 'I don't think so. I'm going to buy baby clothes.'

'For your goddaughter?'

'Yes.'

'I'd still like to come with you. I'll make myself useful and carry the bags. Then we can have lunch and discuss how we're going to work together to win you the support of the Board.'

She gasped. 'Well, if you put it like that…'

Pierre forced himself not to stare at Beth as they rode the lift to the ground floor. He hadn't exaggerated his assessment of her presentation. She'd been backed into a corner and come out fighting. He'd been shocked to hear how well she delivered her plans, and how ably she supported them with facts and figures.

He hadn't given her an opportunity to present her case to him, and that had been a mistake on his part. He admitted it. He'd fallen into the trap of assuming she wouldn't be up to the task because she was young, sweet and pretty. He had to acknowledge this view was ridiculous. She was the same age as him. She'd been around wine people all her life. She'd trained with some of the best in the business. And, as he now knew, she was highly qualified.

He had to admit too that her ideas had merit. Lateral thinking at its best. But still, he would reserve his judgment until they'd gone over everything together. She had, after all, gone out of her way to avoid taking the straightforward route to increasing profitability. There were risks involved in such a strategy. She believed those risks were worth taking because she was ruled by her heart, not her head.

He had yet to be convinced that her plans made sound business sense. He wouldn't change his position until he was convinced. He wouldn't lurch from one mistaken position to another. He would spend time with her, listen to her, give her an opportunity to argue her case. All the things he'd deemed unnecessary when he first arrived.

It would be difficult. It would mean taking an emotional risk—one he had never envisaged when he'd boarded the plane to come here. It might mean opening up a wound that had barely closed, but he didn't have a choice. If he was honest, he didn't want a choice.

Spending time with Beth beckoned like a beacon. He wouldn't trade that opportunity for all the emotional security in the world.

He was like an off-balance tightrope walker. There was nothing he could do but go forward.

Beth glanced at Pierre, standing between a giant teddy bear and a display of foam building blocks. She smothered a smile and turned her attention to the rack of cute dresses. She didn't understand why he'd insisted on joining her, but she couldn't deny feeling a thrill of appreciation that he had. Maurice wouldn't have been caught dead in a baby shop, even for their own child. And that was something she couldn't picture—Maurice and herself as parents. Never would have happened.

Of course Pierre was already a father. Maybe that made the difference. Her stomach tightened at the thought of another woman bearing his child, and she had to pull herself up. There was no sense at all in thinking it should have been her.

She glanced at him again. It seemed to be a day for surprises. She hadn't expected his apology. Most men in his position would have had bruised egos to nurse after having been embarrassed on their own turf—and by a woman. But not Pierre. He'd been more than magnanimous in defeat.

Not that it was a complete win for her. She still had to prove herself to the Board. But she had to admit his behaviour now was more like what she'd have expected from the young Pierre.

But she'd slipped up by revealing her weakness to the

enemy, by admitting she felt like an impostor stepping into her father's shoes. And she couldn't forget how Pierre had tried to manipulate her with that kiss. She closed her eyes till the sudden sharp pain dulled.

Maybe she was wrong to think of him as the enemy now. She did have to work with him to satisfy the Board. And he was right about this being an opportunity for her. If she could persuade him she had everything under control, he would tell the directors her plan was feasible and she'd be home free. What was that old saying about catching flies with honey? She should make an effort to be nice towards him. Persuasion was the way to go. Definitely.

She made her selection, added it to the pile of clothes wedged under her arm, and made her way to Pierre.

'All done.'

'That was quick,' he said.

She glanced up. 'Are you being sarcastic?'

'Of course not.' A smile crept across his face and she wagged a finger at him as they reached the checkout.

'You didn't have to come. It was your choice.'

'I know.' He shrugged. 'Call me a masochist,' he said, with a strange look in his eyes.

Beth didn't know how to react. She had the feeling he wasn't talking about the shopping. She signed the credit card slip and reached for the bulky plastic bag.

'That's my job,' Pierre said, taking the bag from her hand.

His fingers brushed hers and a shockwave shot all the way to her toes. She quickly walked ahead to hide her blush. It took a few minutes to weave their way through the department store before they emerged into the midday heat.

'*Dieu.* It was much more comfortable inside. Are you sure you don't need more baby clothes?'

She chuckled. 'I'm sure. I do need a coffee, though. Shall we find an air-conditioned café and have lunch now?'

'Good idea. What about this one?' He pointed at the café next door to the store they'd just left.

'Okay.'

He pushed the door open and held it for her to enter. Once inside, she could see they'd chosen the wrong place. Or at least the wrong time. City workers on their lunchbreaks crammed into the small space, and the only free table was a tiny one near the door. She sighed and lunged at one of the two chairs. Pierre placed the bag on the other chair, asked her what she'd like to eat, and went to the counter to order.

When he returned with two coffees, Beth moved the bag to the floor, and in order to leave the walkway free had to shuffle her chair up close to Pierre's. With his long legs, the length of his thigh brushed against hers as he sat down. She tensed her abdominal muscles in an effort to stop her stomach leaping.

'So, tell me,' he said. 'Why did Laura Elizabeth's parents choose you as her godmother?'

'We're friends,' she said. 'Our families have been friends for a long time. Karl and I used to play together when we were children.'

'But why did Tasha say you and your father were like saints to the Himmels?'

She wished he hadn't heard that. 'If it hadn't been for my father setting up his winery in the seventies, Karl's father would have lost his vineyard and the family home. You see, he'd committed to selling his entire crop to Box Tree Wines, and he wouldn't have been able to sell it elsewhere at that late stage. Supply exceeded demand that year. Dad bought the lot, of course. If he hadn't, the Himmels would have been ruined.'

Pierre sipped his coffee and watched her over the rim of the cup. 'But there's more to it, isn't there? Tasha said you *and* your father were like saints to them.'

She shifted in her seat. If she told him what had happened the previous year, he would think her a soft touch. Even incompetent.

'Tasha exaggerates.' She picked up her cup and sipped the hot coffee.

'Why don't you want to tell me?'

'It's not that. I…' She sighed. She might as well tell him. If she didn't, he'd no doubt imagine worse. 'Okay. Last year was a really bad one for the Himmels. Their son, Daniel, became sick.' She grimaced, remembering the horror she'd felt when they'd told her just how sick he was. 'It was awful. He needed an operation. A very expensive one.'

She drank a few more sips of coffee. 'They'd let their health insurance lapse because money was tight, and then Corinne had had to give up work to look after Daniel. Without her income, the bank wouldn't consider giving them a loan.' She shrugged. 'They were in a mess.'

'So you helped them? You gave them the money?'

'Not exactly. I…er…paid them in advance for this year's crop.'

She saw the look of surprise spread across his face.

'I didn't use any money from the winery,' she said hastily. 'I took out a loan in my own name. I took the risk myself.'

He nodded. 'That was very generous of you.'

'No.' She shook her head. 'Anyone would have done the same.'

'You think so?' He raised his eyebrows, then his expression changed to one of concern. 'How is the boy?'

'Great.' She brightened. 'He's a normal, healthy nine-year-old. The operation was a complete success. Makes it all worthwhile.'

'Good. And how will the Himmels manage without the income from this year's grapes?'

'Fine.' She bit her lip. She'd shared enough with him, she decided. He didn't need to know about the deal she'd worked out for them.

'I'm starving,' she said. 'Where's our food?'

'It's coming.' He laughed. 'You are extraordinary, Beth.'

She frowned at him. 'You mean weird?'

'No. I mean fascinating. Intriguing.'

'Oh.' Luckily she didn't have to speak for a moment, because the café proprietor arrived at the table with two plates containing their baguettes.

As they began to eat, Beth said, 'Daniel Himmel must be the same age as your son?'

Pierre nodded.

'What's his name?' she asked gently.

He looked up and she saw the sadness in his eyes.

'His name is Philippe.'

'You said you don't see him very often. Is that because of your work?'

'Yes—too much travel. But also because his mother has sole custody.'

'You must have access rights, surely? Visitation?'

He pulled a face. 'Yes, but Arlette makes it as difficult as possible. She's a…' He paused 'Well, in English you would say a bitch.'

Beth waited while a waitress removed their empty coffee cups. 'Where do they live?' she asked.

'Paris.' He grimaced. 'Philippe hates it.'

'Why?'

'Because he's noisy, dirty and sport-obsessed.'

She chuckled. 'Sounds normal for a boy.'

'Exactly. But they live in an elegant Parisian apartment. He's not allowed out on his own, of course, but his mother never takes him to a park—and then she wonders why he runs around inside. He is always in trouble.'

'Poor thing.' Beth frowned. 'It's no life for a young boy, is it?'

Pierre put his baguette down on the plate. 'No, it's not. That's why I have applied for custody. Sole custody, if possible, but joint custody if it's the best I can do. I put things in motion with my lawyer a little while ago. I would have done it sooner, but there was no point without a permanent home base. No court would grant custody to a father who moves around as much as I do. And it's not what I want for Philippe anyway.'

'That's going to change?'

He nodded. 'As soon as I finish this assignment I'll be able to take up a permanent posting in France. It's what I've been waiting for. I have to live in France to have a chance of winning the custody case, and I have to win. For Philippe's sake…and my own.'

Beth's heart lurched at the intensity in his tone. She wished she could help. 'You really miss him, don't you?'

He nodded. 'A great deal.' He looked up and his eyes locked on hers. 'He reminds me of you, Beth.'

She gasped.

'Not as far as looks are concerned. Actually, he looks very much like I did as a child.' He shrugged. 'No, it's his enthusiasm for everything he does.'

'Are you saying I'm childish?' she asked, not sure whether to be insulted.

'No. Well…' He tapped his chin thoughtfully. 'Yes, but not in a bad way. I was referring to your love of life. It is a child-like quality, and I don't mean anything derogatory by it. It's a large part of your charm.'

His words caused her stomach to churn like a washing machine.

'On the other hand, you were very much a mature woman when you spoke to the Board this morning,' he went on. 'A commanding presence.'

She broke into a broad smile. 'I'm glad you thought so.'

Chewing on her sandwich, she took a moment to assimilate this new information. If his son reminded him of her, did that mean he'd thought of her over the years when he'd looked at Philippe? And, particularly in light of his failed marriage, had he regretted what he'd done to her? She hoped so. She hoped he'd thought about what they'd had, and hoped he'd suffered from the agony of knowing he'd wrecked it. Though no amount of suffering on his part could come close to hers.

CHAPTER TEN

THEIR return journey felt very different from the drive into the city that morning. Then, they'd both been reserved—sullen, even—speaking only when absolutely necessary.

Something had changed, Beth knew. Her performance for the Board seemed to have given Pierre a new-found respect for her and her opinions. Had she really made such an impression? And, if so, why hadn't she made the effort to demonstrate her ability earlier?

She knew the answer was wrapped up in her own feelings of inadequacy. Frank Asper's and Pierre's views hadn't been too far removed from her own. Although for different reasons.

They'd considered her an unqualified woman with no experience of the business world. She'd known she had the qualifications to equal any candidate they could put forward, but she'd still doubted her right to be there. She wasn't her father. Simple as that. How could she possibly follow in his legendary footsteps? Respected and revered throughout the industry. An icon. And what was she? An ungrateful daughter who'd let him down when he needed her most.

Beth sighed silently. She had to get past her hang-ups. Even though he wasn't there, her father needed her now. And he'd trusted her to do what had to be done. Trusted her to save his winery so it would be there for future generations of his family—though she didn't know where they were going to come from. Simon's descendants maybe? Owen's? The chances of *her* becoming a mother were remote to non-existent.

Shaking her head to scatter those thoughts, she brought her focus back to the task at hand. She knew what she had to do. She had to make the most of Pierre's turnaround. With him in such a receptive mood, she'd have a chance of convincing him her plans for the business were the right ones. If the directors wanted re-assurance they would be making a safe decision before giving her their backing, she'd make sure they had it. She'd communicate her ideas fully to Pierre, so he could make an accurate evaluation. She had enough confidence in her business plan to believe it would be positive. Rather than holding back, as she had since his arrival, she'd go all out to impress him.

She parked in front of The Barn. When they'd converted more buildings like this one they'd make a respectable income from hiring them out as tourist accommodation. It was lucky The Barn had been empty this week—

Damn. She'd forgotten it was only free for one week. And that week was up. Now what was she going to do?

'Um, Pierre?'

He'd opened the car door, and with one foot already on the ground he smiled back at her.

'I've just remembered,' she said. 'The Barn is booked

for the next week. I'm afraid we'll have to move you out by mid-morning tomorrow.'

'Ah.' He glanced up at The Barn and back at Beth. 'What do you suggest as an alternative?'

She thought quickly. If they hired any of the local cottages he'd be distant from the winery just when she needed him to take more interest in it. What about Tasha or Owen? Could one of them put him up?

She chewed her lip. Owen's wife hadn't been well of late, so it didn't seem fair to ask him. And Tasha had been a bit quiet about Pierre since the night he'd eaten at her house. Beth wondered if they'd argued. She didn't think it would be a great idea to throw them together anyway, and she wasn't going to examine that decision too closely.

She could invite him to move into her own house. Space wasn't a problem. On the other hand, having Pierre share her home might be. But she could tough it out. She had to. It wouldn't be for long, and it was for the winery.

'Perhaps I could pitch a tent on the lawn down there?' He pointed towards the picnic area in front of the old cottage.

Beth choked back a bubble of laughter. 'We can do better than that.' She hesitated, then rushed ahead. 'Would you mind moving into my house?'

His eyes opened wide. 'Are you sure?'

'Well, it seems logical. I have spare rooms, and it makes sense for you to stay close by so we can work together, like you said.'

He shrugged. 'Thank you. I would be pleased to do so.'

She exhaled. 'It's settled, then. If you could move your things out by, say, ten o'clock tomorrow morning, it will give me time to clean before the next guests arrive.'

'I'll help you.'

She flapped a hand. 'No.'

He lifted his shoulders. 'It is my dirt.'

'True.' She bit her bottom lip. 'Okay, if you insist. I'll meet you here.'

He got out of the car and she started the engine, then thought of something else. 'About dinner tonight?'

He crouched down to her level. 'Yes?'

'I've been invited to eat at the Himmels, so I can see little Laura. I'm sure they wouldn't mind if you came along too—if you'd like to, that is.'

'I wouldn't want to make extra work for them with a new baby in the house.'

'No, it's fine. It's just going to be a barbecue in the back garden. I'll take some extra meat. Between us, the guests are providing all the food, so you don't need to worry about making work. Tasha will be there, so you'll know one other person.'

'Tasha?' He frowned.

'What? Have you two had words?'

'Words? You mean an argument? No. But I think I might have…' He grimaced. 'Disappointed her.'

'How?'

He cleared his throat. 'I didn't intend to say anything, but the truth is she asked me to…to…'

Beth held up a hand. 'No, don't tell me. I shouldn't have asked.' She put the car into gear as heat made its way up her throat and into her cheeks.

'I turned her down.'

She absorbed what he'd said. 'You turned her down?'

'Yes, of course.'

Though glad to hear he hadn't slept with her best friend, she felt for Tasha. She must have been devastated. It would have taken all her courage to…do whatever she'd done. Beth knew for a fact she hadn't slept with a man since the death of her husband. And then to be rejected…

'Poor Tash. How did she take it?'

'She seemed…upset.' She saw concern in his eyes. 'I tried not to be hurtful but…' He gave a what-else-could-I-do? shrug.

'I'm sure you did. Even so, she must have been humiliated.' She sighed. 'But Tasha is a strong person. She's probably over you already.'

He smiled. 'I hope so.'

The warmth of his smile melted a tiny corner of the solid lump of pain she'd grown used to carrying inside. She smiled back. 'About the barbecue—you will come, won't you?'

That evening, Beth tugged at Tasha's sleeve and they tiptoed out of Laura Elizabeth's room.

'She's beautiful,' Tasha whispered.

'Absolutely.' Beth ushered her friend across the passageway into the deserted lounge room. 'Tash, I hope you don't mind me bringing Pierre here tonight?'

'No. Why should I?'

'Because he told me what happened at your house.'

Tasha's face flushed. 'The rat. Is he going around telling everyone?'

'No—no, of course not,' Beth said quickly. 'He explained to me why he didn't think he'd be welcome here tonight. That's all.'

'Hmmph.'

'I told him not to worry about it. I said you'd be over him already. Was I right?'

'Pretty much.'

Beth sighed. 'I'm glad. You *will* meet someone who's right for you, Tash. I know you will.'

'There you are.' Corinne Himmel stood in the doorway. 'I wondered where you'd got to. Is Laura still asleep?'

'Yes,' Beth said. 'She's waiting for the right moment to make her grand entrance.'

The other two women grinned, and the three of them made their way to the lawn behind the Himmels' house. Beth saw Pierre as soon as she stepped outside. She allowed herself a moment to enjoy the sight of him. Dressed in olive-green cotton trousers and a lemon polo shirt, he looked gorgeous. But it was the smile on his face that made her chest ache.

'Beth?'

She started, then smiled down at Daniel Himmel. 'Hi, Danny. What are you up to?'

'Making a treehouse.'

'A treehouse? Sounds interesting. Where is it?'

'Round the corner,' he said, pointing to the side garden. 'Do you want to see it?'

'I'd love to.'

Daniel ran off, and Beth followed him at a fast walk, trying to maintain her dignity. What the heck? she thought. There wasn't much to maintain. And she began to run. With her longer legs, she soon caught up with her young friend.

'Oh, wow, this is fantastic, Danny.' She looked up at the wooden structure about three metres from the ground in a sturdy red-gum. It had been made by a skilled carpenter, not a nine-year-old boy. That much was obvious. 'Er, did your dad help you?'

'Well, yes, but he said he wouldn't have been able to do it without me. Come on, you have to see inside.'

Secure in the knowledge it was Karl's handiwork, Beth climbed the ladder behind Daniel and crawled through a low opening clearly meant to deter adults. She looked around at the contents of the treehouse and grinned. He'd lined the walls with coloured pictures of sporting heroes and stacked his treasured cricket gear in one corner. A pile of comics and a Game Boy were the only other contents.

'Beth?' Pierre's voice came from the ground below.

Beth and Daniel looked at each other and she touched a fingertip to her lips. Daniel nodded.

She crawled to the window in the side wall and looked out. She could see Pierre shading his eyes as he gazed around. Without thinking, Beth let out a low wolf-whistle, then ducked down below the window ledge. Daniel started to giggle, and she made frantic gestures at him to be quiet—which only made him laugh more. She rolled her eyes when Pierre's head appeared at the top of the ladder.

'Knock-knock?' he said.

'Who's there?' Daniel said, then collapsed in giggles.

She saw Pierre's face soften as he watched Daniel,

and her heart seemed to turn over in her chest. If only she could see him with his own son.

'Can I come in?' he asked.

Daniel leapt to move a pile of comics so Pierre could sit on the floor with them. 'What do you think of my treehouse?'

'It's one of the best I have ever seen,' Pierre said. 'Every boy should have a treehouse.'

'Did you have one?'

'Yes. I spent a lot of time in it.'

It was on the tip of Beth's tongue to ask whether Philippe had one, but common sense told her he didn't. It wouldn't be possible in a Parisian apartment. She guessed it was one of the things Pierre wanted to remedy.

'Were you looking for me?' she asked.

He looked sheepish. 'I wondered where you were running off to. I was being—what is it?—a sticky nose?'

Beth laughed. 'A sticky beak.'

'Right.'

'Are you from another planet?' Daniel blurted.

Pierre turned a surprised face to him. 'No. Why?'

'Because you talk funny, and you don't know all the words we humans use.'

Pierre chuckled. 'I'm from another country. France. Do you know where it is?'

'Oh, yeah. Dad showed me on the map when the World Cup was on. So, why don't you know about sticky beaks?'

'You Australians use some strange expressions. Most other people in the world don't use them.'

'Excuse me, but you French know all about strange expressions,' Beth said. 'What about *mon petit chou*? Since when was being called a cabbage a term of endearment?'

Daniel yelled with laughter and jumped up. 'I'm going to tell my dad that one,' he said, and disappeared down the ladder before Beth had even thought about moving.

She grinned across at Pierre. 'He's quick, isn't he?'

He nodded. 'He seems very healthy.'

'Yes. He is now. Well, we'd better go too.'

Pierre made no move to leave, and Beth didn't want to squeeze past him. The air inside the small room suddenly seemed taut with tension. He closed the small space between them. 'Or…'

She should move aside, she told herself. But she froze. Anticipation made her pulse pound in her ears, muffling the sound of the barbecue guests. Logic fled as he leaned over and placed his lips lightly against hers. He pulled away. She gave a little whimper and followed him. Then she gasped, her lips only millimetres from his, as she realised what she'd done.

'Beth?'

His whisper made her jump, and she jerked backwards, but his arms went around her and prevented her moving away. He pulled her against him and she let him. Then his mouth found hers in a kiss that rocked her with its desperation and its tenderness. The combination made her body throb. And there was something very erotic about tasting her own wine on his lips.

She would be flooded with regrets, she knew. Later. For now, the only thing flooding through her was desire.

At the sound of footsteps on the ladder they separated—and only just in time, as Daniel's head popped in through the hole.

'Mum said to tell you Laura's awake now,' he said.

'Right.' Beth's voice came out as a squeak.

Daniel ducked out of sight and she turned her head slowly. Pierre stared back at her, looking as astonished as she felt. Their kiss had both aroused her and left her reeling. She tried to ground herself in reality—tried to consider what had happened with cold, hard logic.

This time she didn't suspect him of plotting to mess with her mind. She could see he was as shaken as her. And the circumstances were different now. If anything, she was the one who could be accused of trying to influence him. Of using her feminine wiles to shape his report to the Board. Except she hadn't. She didn't have wiles, for God's sake. That kiss hadn't been the fault of either one of them. It had come from nowhere.

She moistened her lips. 'We should go,' she said.

He nodded, and made his way down the ladder first, waiting to catch her when she hopped off the lowest rung.

She groaned as she twisted in his arms to face him. She wanted to move back, to put some space between them, but she couldn't. She could feel his warm breath on her cheek, could have poked out her tongue and touched his lips. But she wouldn't. Nor would she kiss him again. Though the urge to do so made her ache. She couldn't allow herself to be sucked in to the quagmire that was a relationship with Pierre.

There was no future in it. He had to live in France.

He'd told her so. Nothing was more important to him than his son. She'd seen it in his face, heard it in his voice.

She, on the other hand, would never leave Lowland Wines. Assuming the Board supported her and she retained control, she would devote the rest of her life to ensuring her father's dream lived on.

'I can't do this.'

Pierre let go of her, but continued to stare into her eyes.

Daniel ran towards them with a soccer ball tucked under his arm. 'We're going to have a game,' he called to Pierre. 'The men. While the women look at baby Laura.' He gave Beth a smug look.

The tension that had held her riveted shattered into pieces as she tore her eyes from Pierre's and looked at Daniel. She watched Pierre walk with him to the make-shift soccer pitch, and shook her head at what she'd allowed to happen, before heading off to join the women in the shade of a large eucalyptus.

'Where did you get to?' Tasha asked as Beth crunched across a carpet of gum leaves.

She flopped into a large wooden chair. 'Danny showed me his treehouse.'

'Pierre too?'

'Mmm. Now, where's my gorgeous goddaughter?'

Tasha knew her well, and she could feel her assessing gaze while she cuddled the baby. Excited yells carried to them across the lawn, and Beth swivelled in her chair to see six males of assorted sizes tearing around after Daniel's soccer ball. It looked and sounded like fun.

Laura wailed and claimed Beth's attention. Eventually she admitted defeat and handed her back to Corinne. 'Sorry. I don't have the touch.'

'You will,' Corinne said. 'When you have your own. It will come naturally.'

As Pierre made his way to the group under the tree, he saw Beth hand the tiny baby over to the woman he'd been introduced to earlier. The sight of Beth holding a baby sent a wave of warmth rolling through him, and he had to take a steadying breath before covering the last stretch of ground.

He didn't know what had come over him in the tree-house. He'd had no intention of kissing her again. He'd intended to keep well away from any such contact—especially after what had happened the last time. They'd barely been on speaking terms afterwards. But she'd broken down his defences without even trying.

Who was he trying to fool? He didn't have any defences when it came to her.

The beauty of it was, he hadn't imagined her response. It was as real as the nose on his face. But she was right when she said she couldn't do this. *They* couldn't do this. It was stupid. Ridiculous.

If anything happened between them it would never be a light-hearted fling. He knew himself too well to think he could ever contemplate a short-lived affair with Beth. Yet how could they possibly have anything else? He couldn't stay here, and he couldn't ask her to move to France.

As the male contingent joined the group of women, he pulled up a chair next to Beth's, hoping they would be able to get past the awkwardness of what had happened earlier.

She smiled as she saw him, filling him with relief. 'Good game?' she asked.

He nodded, then started as Karl shoved a cold bottle of beer into his hand. Pierre thanked him, and when he'd walked away looked at Beth, perplexed. 'What am I supposed to do with this?'

'Drink it,' she said. 'It's an Aussie tradition—sport and cold beer go together, even amongst wine people. Do your best.'

He took a swig and grimaced.

She laughed.

The sound went right to his heart. There was nothing else like it.

Two hours later, Beth did the round of her friends, saying goodbye as she prepared to leave the barbecue. As she'd expected, Karl and Corinne and the others had made Pierre welcome, and he'd fitted in well once he'd let down his initial barriers. Finally they left, and walked to the car together. Beth slid behind the steering wheel, closed her door and smiled across at him.

'Did you enjoy it?'

He looked at her, his eyes dark and intense. 'Did you?'

She'd meant the barbecue in general, but she knew Pierre had zeroed in on one brief and specific moment.

'Pierre…'

He sighed. 'I know what you're going to say.'

She gave him a questioning look.

'You're going to tell me you didn't mean it to happen. That it was a big mistake.'

'Well…actually—'

'I understand, Beth. I didn't mean it to happen either. It was the furthest thing from my mind until that moment. I know we can't do this. I'd be an idiot to think we could. It won't happen again.'

She tried to squash the disappointment welling up in her stomach. 'Okay.'

She hadn't had to lay down the law, or beg him to leave her alone. She'd got the result she wanted. So why did it leave her feeling so empty?

CHAPTER ELEVEN

BETH carried the cleaning equipment outside. She'd never enjoyed the chore of cleaning so much. Pierre had already taken his bags outside, and he turned to take the mop and bucket from her.

'Is there anything else to do?'

'No. We've finished.' She flicked one last glance around the spacious room, from the basket of local produce on the kitchen bench to the fresh flowers she'd placed on each coffee table. Their perfume mingled with lemon-scented floor cleaner and beeswax furniture polish. Satisfied, she shut the door. 'Let's go.'

They walked slowly down the hill in the hot sun, Beth pushing the trolley and Pierre carrying his bags.

'You have quite a diverse job, don't you?' Pierre said. 'Not many people could switch between international marketing and cleaning in the same day.'

'I suppose you think I should hire someone to do it, but I've never seen the point. I enjoy making The Barn welcoming for guests. It might be different in the future, of course.'

If she had a future here.

'You mean, when you've quadrupled the number of guesthouses?'

'Yes. I thought we'd drive over to the old farm, so you can see the buildings we're planning to convert. What do you think?'

He nodded. 'How long will it take?'

'Let's see—half an hour maximum, each way. Half an hour to look around. Why?'

'Perhaps we should take a picnic lunch?'

Her stomach gurgled at the thought of food. And at the thought of having a picnic lunch with Pierre. But a picnic didn't have to be romantic. It could be whatever they made it.

'Good idea,' she said. 'I'll prepare a picnic while you settle into your room.'

'No, I'll do it while you shower and change your clothes.' He glanced at her. 'I assume you *do* intend to change?'

She chuckled. 'Yes. Even *I* don't go out and about looking like this.' She indicated her outfit with a wave of her hand. Her old bleach-spattered track pants and baggy T-shirt were comfortable for cleaning but not suitable for being seen in. It hadn't occurred to her to worry about what Pierre thought of her outfit, and the realisation gave her a jolt. Was she so comfortable with him? When had that happened?

Inside the house, she showed him to the room that was to be his for the remainder of his stay and stood to one side while he placed his case on the bed. Then she pointed out the bathroom and lounge room on the way to the kitchen.

'I'll get the Esky,' she said, opening a tall built-in cupboard.

'The *what*?'

She turned with the icebox in her hand. 'The Esky.' She tapped the lid. 'For the picnic.'

'Right.'

'I'll leave you to it, then—if you're sure? There's ice in the freezer, and food in the fridge and the pantry.' She pointed to a door in the corner of the room. 'Have fun.'

In the shower, Beth wondered whether she'd done the right thing, inviting him into her house, but shook off her concern. It was too late now to worry about it. She could hardly ask him to move out again. And surely she could control her feelings for a few days? Well, she'd have to.

She dressed in one of her favourite floaty, floral skirts, with a white peasant-style top which she thought Pierre would like. As soon as she had the thought she pushed it away. She dressed to please herself.

Pierre snapped the Esky lid closed as she entered the kitchen, and his hand froze above the handle while his eyes raked over her. For a moment she thought she'd made the wrong choice, but then his eyes connected with hers and she saw the gleam in them. She swallowed hard, banking down her body's response to that gleam.

He broke into a smile. 'Ready to go?'

The old farm lay on the far side of the Lowland Wines property and Beth took the long way round, driving through Nuriootpa, a town with a more bustling atmosphere and a less apparent European heritage than any other town in the valley. In Nuri, as it was known to the locals, Beth found herself waving at acquaintances almost non-stop.

'Do you know *everyone* here?' Pierre asked.

'Pretty much.' She grinned as an old friend of her father's tipped his hat at her. 'Do you know much about the history of the Valley?' she asked as they left the town behind.

'Nothing—except there has been a strong German influence.' He looked at her, eyebrows raised. 'Are you going to enlighten me?'

'If you want me to.'

'Yes. I like to hear your voice.'

'Oh.' Beth gulped. 'Yes, well. Okay. It's different from any other part of Australia in the way it was settled,' she said. 'An entire community transplanted itself here from Silesia. They were Lutherans escaping from religious persecution at the hands of the King of Prussia.'

Pierre half turned in his seat, his head tilted to the side. She felt her skin prickle as he watched her face. She wished she could turn off her awareness of him, but, especially in the confined space of the car, she had no chance. She took a deep breath.

'The pastor who led the migration has been called the Moses of his people.'

He nodded.

'The migrants brought cuttings of vines with them and established vineyards, as well as farms just big enough to sustain their families. So, the Barossa became a patchwork of different grape varieties and viticultural practices—as it still is, to a large extent. It was an orderly, hardworking community, and many of the people who live here now are direct descendants of the original migrants.'

'Karl Himmel, for instance?'

'Yes.' She smiled. 'So you can see, I hope, why I had to help the Himmels last year. I mean, I would have done what I could for the sake of our friendship, but it goes further than that.'

'I do see, Beth. You don't have to justify your action. It was the right thing to do. Risky, but right.'

She beamed at him for as long as she dared take her eyes from the road. The Pierre who would have criticised her sentimentality had skedaddled back to wherever he'd come from, and he'd left behind the compassionate person she'd first known.

'That's good to hear,' she said. Very, very good.

He shrugged. 'Perhaps I'm not as heartless as you think me.'

Further on, they veered off the sealed road, and after a little while turned into a winding driveway.

'What are these buildings?' Pierre asked when she'd parked the car.

'There was a small farm here. I'm not sure when it fell into disuse, but it was some time before my father bought the land. They haven't been used since then, as far as I know.'

She waited till they were walking towards the first cottage before continuing her explanation. 'Apparently an extended family lived here, and built three separate cottages so they weren't all under each other's feet. There's also a barn, and another building which I'll show you in a little while.'

She pushed open the front door. 'Obviously all the buildings will have to be gutted and completely refurbished, but the important thing is to retain the original shell. People from the city like to stay in such old buildings. They like the solidity of the stone and the history surrounding each building. But at the same time, naturally, they like their home comforts.'

'The refurbishment will be expensive,' Pierre said as he gazed around the dilapidated house.

She shrugged. 'Not as much as you might think. People like Clive and John are very versatile. They can do a lot of the work without bringing in outsiders, as they did on The Barn. Except for the licensed trades, of course. And I can do most of the decorating myself. Tasha will help, and other friends will pitch in too.'

They walked on to the next building and Beth led the way inside.

'I have all the costings back at the office. I'll show you. You'll be surprised.'

'And what makes you think people will want to stay here?'

She walked back outside and made an expansive gesture with her arms. 'All of this. The view. The smell.' She paused to breathe in deeply. 'The sound of the birds. The fresh air. You don't get all of this in the city. And then there's the freedom. They'll be free to wander through the vines and walk wherever the fancy takes them.

'The location is great, because it's completely private, but it's not far off the beaten track, and the road passing by here is one of the main tourist drives. Short holidays and long weekends are very popular with busy people who don't have the time to travel interstate or overseas.'

She started walking around the outside of the cottage and motioned for him to follow her. 'Just look at the view from the back of the house.'

With hands on hips, she stood gazing out. Vines stretched ahead, and to her left a creek tumbled over rocks and a flock of chattering lorikeets rose up from the clump of trees along one bank.

Hills formed a backdrop to the vines and changed colour as a cloud passed in front of the sun. She sighed. 'Gorgeous, isn't it? Can you imagine spending a weekend here after a stressful week in the city?'

'Yes. You make a good case.' He stood for a moment, eyes on the view, then he turned to her. 'Now, what about this other building you mentioned?'

'Ah, yes.' She pointed at a low stone building with two pairs of double doors. 'Over there.'

She set off towards it, and Pierre strode along beside her. 'What we're going to do is divide it into two.' With his help, she tugged open one of the heavy warped doors. 'And then one half of the building will be hired to Karl Himmel. He's going to use it as an outlet for his wood-carving and cabinet-making business. He's incredibly talented, and he's already getting lots of enquiries.'

'Why not open up on his own land?'

'He doesn't have a large building like this, so the start-up cost is prohibitive.'

'The other half?'

'To be rented to Clive Bauer's wife, Jenny. She's started making a range of cheeses and other products—

ice cream, cheesecakes and so on. At the moment she takes the food to the farmers' market at Angaston, but it's only on once a week and she sells out within a couple of hours. She needs a larger kitchen, where she can expand, and then she can start supplying local shops and restaurants as well.'

'What about the kitchen equipment?'

'Jenny will pay for anything that isn't a permanent fixture. Again, it's all been costed, and I'll show you later. And having Karl and Jenny here during the day will be good if the guests have any problems—they'll be only too happy to help. They'll provide tourist info and answer queries.' She rammed the door back into place and smiled. 'I'm keen to hear your initial reaction.'

He looked serious, and she drew in a sharp breath.

'It's not core winemaking business, I know,' she said. 'But I believe diversification of this type is greatly preferable to destroying the quality of the wines by increasing production.'

The corners of his mouth curled up. 'I would like to reserve my judgement till I've seen the figures. I am a risk management specialist, after all. But my instinct tells me the figures will be good. I think you are an incredible woman, Beth. Very enterprising.'

'Does this mean you'll make a positive report to the Board?'

'Let's not get ahead of ourselves.' He smiled to soften his words.

'Of course.' She nodded. She fully understood he had to see the figures before committing himself, but he was on her side now. She could feel it. And it felt great.

'Are you hungry?' he asked.

'Famished.'

'Good. My first effort at preparing a picnic won't be wasted, then.'

'Definitely not.'

They chose a suitable spot near one of the cottages, and spread the blanket in a generous patch of shade courtesy of an ancient camphor laurel tree. Pierre placed the Esky in the centre. When Beth went to open it, he stopped her.

'No. It's my turn to serve you today.'

'But…'

He opened the Esky and took out two plates, two glasses and a bottle of wine.

'Okay.' She settled down, leaning back against the tree trunk. 'I hope you remembered to pack a cork-screw. We haven't changed to screw-tops yet.'

He rolled his eyes. 'Do you think I would forget, with *my* background?'

She chuckled. 'No, I suppose not.'

He passed her a glass of the chilled Chardonnay, and while she sipped it took a plastic box full of sandwiches from the Esky and offered it to her.

'Mmm, they look good…for a first effort.'

He grinned. 'Perhaps I'll progress to cooking soon.'

She looked at him as she ate her sandwich. He seemed so much more relaxed than when he'd first arrived. 'That's the second time you've mentioned learning to cook. Do you miss your mother's cooking?'

He turned a surprised face to her. 'No. It's not that.'

'Why, then?'

'I will need to show I am capable of looking after Philippe if I—*when* I win custody of him. The court will not give him to me if they think I'm incapable of fulfilling his basic needs.' His expression darkened. 'They won't be able to see how much better that would be than leaving him with Arlette. She manages the basics, after a fashion, but nothing else. She does not look after him well.'

'She doesn't?'

He shook his head and, much as she hated to think of him with Arlette, she wondered what kind of marriage they'd had.

'She doesn't care about his happiness,' he said bitterly. 'She starves him of affection.'

She gazed at him for a moment. 'That's awful. Poor Philippe. No wonder you're desperate to take him away from her.'

He nodded. 'Desperate is the right word. My son's happiness comes first now. I won't let anything get in its way. Not my own needs. Nothing.'

Beth took a sip of wine. If she'd needed confirmation that there was no future for them, she'd just had it. All the more reason to be careful around him. She didn't have children, but she would like to think she'd be as determined to do something about it if they were in the same situation as Philippe. She understood his determination. And she certainly wouldn't do anything to make it more difficult for him.

'Pierre, can I ask you something personal?'

He looked wary, but gave her a slight nod.

'Didn't you know what Arlette was like when you married her?'

'Well, no.' He shrugged. 'I hardly knew her.'

'Then why marry her?'

He took a drink of wine and carefully balanced the half-empty glass on the ground. 'Beth, this is not easy for me to talk about.'

She gasped. 'Do you think it's easy for me to ask?'

He stared at her for a moment, then rubbed his eyes with the thumb and forefinger of his free hand.

'I married Arlette because she asked me. Sounds pathetic, doesn't it?' He stopped, picked up the glass again, and emptied it in one long drink.

Beth was conscious of a chill creeping through her veins. She didn't speak. After examining his empty glass for a long moment, Pierre went on.

'I had been acquainted with her for years, of course. As the daughter of a neighbouring vineyard owner, she was always around. But I didn't know her as well as I knew—'

He broke off and tipped his head back for a moment. Beth saw him swallow several times. She should stop him, change the subject. But she couldn't. She wanted to hear what he had to say.

'When you left,' he said eventually, 'I knew I would never love again, so I agreed to Arlette's timely proposal.'

Beth twitched violently, knocking her glass over. She stared at the wine soaking into the blanket. Neither she nor Pierre made a move to clean it up. Beth's chest tightened. She had thought he'd fallen for the sophisticated brunette because she was everything Beth wasn't. Everything he needed.

'You didn't love Arlette?' she asked.

'Of course not,' he said in a disgusted tone. 'I thought, since I'd never marry for love, I should at least give my parents the grandchild they wanted.' He sighed. 'To ensure the winery would always remain in the family.'

He laughed, but there was no humour in the sound. 'Ironic. I gave my father the grandchild he wanted, and he gave the winery away.'

She winced at the bitterness in his voice. His hurt ran deep. 'Why did the marriage break up?'

He stared out over the vines. 'We should never have married.' After a moment he glanced at her, then turned away again. 'I thought I could make it work, but a marriage that is not based on love is doomed from the start.'

All the tightly held anger and hurt inside her drove Beth to her feet. She crossed the bare ground till she reached the vines. She wasn't the only one who'd suffered as a result of Pierre's decision to stay in France all those years ago. He hadn't had such a great time himself. Arlette hadn't deserved a loveless marriage. But, more importantly, there was Philippe, an innocent child. She heard the crunch of footsteps behind her and swung around to face him.

'Why didn't you just come to Australia with me? Then none of this would have happened.'

His stricken look almost made her back up.

'Oh, Beth.' He lifted his hands, then dropped them again. 'I couldn't.'

'Why not?'

He rubbed his forehead. 'That was when I found out about the state of the winery. About my father's total lack of business sense. It was clear that if I didn't do something about it we would lose the whole thing. I tried my best, but I was young. I didn't know enough about business back then. And in truth it was too late. But I didn't know that. I had to try.'

Beth covered her mouth with her hand.

'What would you have done in my place?' he asked. 'The same, I'm sure.'

Of course she would. 'But why didn't you *tell* me? I thought you didn't love me enough to give up your comfortable life in France.'

'You thought that?' He shrugged his shoulders in a bewildered gesture. His arms hung limply at his sides. 'I don't know how you could have done. Wasn't it obvious how much I loved you?'

'No. Not when you changed your mind about coming back with me. I mean, we had it all arranged. We'd made plans. Then you simply said you couldn't do it.'

'But I asked you to stay.'

'Yes, which just went to show that you only wanted me on *your* terms. Why the hell didn't you tell me what was going on? You must have known I'd understand.'

He hesitated. 'I was too hurt when you refused to stay. You'd made your decision. My pride was all I had left. I didn't want to beg.'

'Beg?' She shook her head in disbelief. 'I would have stayed in a heartbeat.' A deep ache for all they'd missed out on reverberated through her bones.

Pierre reached for her arm but she flinched, moving out of his reach. He swore in French and aimed a kick at a stone near his foot. When he lifted his head, the raw anguish in his face took her breath away. She knew he was having the same thoughts. Without intending to, she stepped towards him and he pulled her into his arms. They clung to each other.

CHAPTER TWELVE

WITH her face buried in Pierre's chest, Beth breathed deeply, savouring the scent of his skin through the thin cotton of his shirt. Slowly she raised her head and looked into his eyes. Emotion flowed between them, and as he bent his head she stretched up to meet him halfway. His lips touched hers like a whisper, then gently covered her mouth in a delicate caress. She felt and shared his amazement, his disbelief at their discovery, as his mouth moved softly over hers.

All these years they'd each believed the other guilty of not loving enough. And now they were no closer to spending the rest of their lives together than before they'd discovered the truth.

Her lips trembled when he pulled away. Neither spoke. He stared at her, his dark eyes smouldering, and she watched as emotions played across his face. Then he recaptured her mouth, his kiss more urgent this time. It stirred the stored-up passion of a decade apart, and desire surged through her bloodstream.

She gripped his shoulders while his hands slid over her back, her arms, her hips. Every touch sent shivers spiralling through her. And when his hand moved inside her blouse, to caress the bare skin of her back, she thought her nerve-endings would explode.

It had been so long since she'd felt heat rushing through her body like this, urging her on. Her pulse pounded in her ears, her knees trembled, and only with a supreme effort did she manage to retreat from the brink of surrendering to delicious sensation. But she did. As his fingertips slipped under the lace of her bra, she let out a cry of anguish.

He stepped back at once and held up his hands, horror painted on his face. '*Dieu.* I'm sorry.'

She wrapped her arms around her waist. 'No, Pierre. Don't apologise. I wanted you to touch me. More than anything. I've waited so long.'

Frustration raged inside her, but she fought it, and when Pierre stepped forward again she held up her hands to fend him off.

'But this is too sudden. I can't do this. Not now. Maybe not at all.'

Her voice caught in her throat and she looked at him with a silent appeal for understanding. She needed time to work all this out in her head before she could follow her heart.

He nodded slowly. 'I won't rush you.' He pushed his hands into his pockets. 'Besides, this time is different. I'm not young and impetuous any more. I have some self-control.'

He held her gaze, and the look in his eyes reached right to her soul. 'When we make love,' he said, 'I want to be sure it's because you want to. Not because of any pressure from me.'

She swallowed. Her heart ached with suppressed love for him.

'If,' she said shakily. 'Not when. If.'

Tasha had customers when Beth entered the cottage late in the afternoon. She perched on a high stool at the end of the counter and listened to Tasha's smooth spiel. The two couples appeared knowledgeable, and were clearly keen to buy. Beth glanced around the cottage. Very much Tasha's domain, she kept it spotless as well as welcoming.

Leaving the customers to make their final selection, Tasha nipped across to her. 'Hey, Beth. Where have you been all day?'

'Out.'

'Well, thanks for solving that mystery.'

'Sorry. I didn't mean to be obtuse. I've been showing Pierre around the old farm. He was interested to see the buildings we're going to convert for accommodation. Tash,' she said, touching her friend's forearm, 'I have something to tell you.'

'Ooh—something juicy, I hope. Just a second.' Tasha returned to her customers, and Beth heard her congratulate them on an excellent choice.

A few minutes later Tasha placed a coffee in front of Beth and settled herself on a stool on the other side of the counter. 'Okay,' she said between sips. 'Tell all.'

'Well…'

Tasha's expression became serious at the struggle Beth was having to get the words out. 'Are you sick?'

'No! It's nothing like that. I promise.'

'So, come on. Spit it out.'

Beth took a deep breath. 'You know I said I met Pierre when I was in France?'

'Yup.'

'I didn't tell you the whole truth. You see, we were in love.'

Tasha sputtered coffee onto the counter. She jumped up to grab a box of tissues. 'Oh…my…God,' she said as she cleaned up. 'Well, that explains…quite a few things, actually. Why didn't you tell me?'

'I didn't know you back then.'

'Sure, but what about now? What about when you heard he was coming over? Why did you pretend there was nothing between you?'

'Oh, I don't know, Tash. It was a very painful experience, and one I'd tried hard to forget for years, so when I heard he was coming here the last thing I wanted to do was rake it up again.'

'Right.' Tasha gave her a sympathetic look before dropping the tissues in the bin under the counter. 'So why are you telling me now? I assume something has happened?'

Beth nodded. 'Today, we talked for the first time about the past. It turns out we could have avoided all the hurt if we hadn't both been too proud to really communicate.'

'You're kidding!'

'Oh, yes. I always joke about having my heart broken.'

Tasha slid back onto her stool, looking thoughtful. 'I thought there was something in the way he looked at you…'

'What sort of something?'

'Oh, you know. Like his eyes went all misty and soft.'

Beth chuckled. 'I don't believe you.'

Tasha shrugged. 'Up to you. So, he's going to move here now, is he?'

Beth's face fell. 'No. That's why I'm here. I want to talk to you.'

'You *are* talking to me.'

Beth chewed on her lip. 'Remember he mentioned having a son?'

'Yes.'

'He's hoping to win custody. More than hoping. It's the most important thing in the world to him.'

'Geez, that'll be hard, won't it? Courts won't take a child from its mother without very good reason.'

Beth nodded. 'He might have to settle for joint custody.'

Tasha tilted her head to one side, her eyes narrowed. 'And?'

'Even if he wins sole custody, his ex-wife will have visitation rights.'

'Ye-es?'

'Which means he will have to live in France.' Beth closed her eyes as a spear of pain shot through her. She felt Tasha's hand on hers, squeezing, and she fought to keep tears from forcing their way between her eyelids.

'You wouldn't leave Lowland Wines, would you?'

Beth shook her head. Her eyes opened slowly. 'You know I wouldn't. I promised Dad. I let him down too many times in the past. I couldn't live with myself if I did it again.'

She looked at her friend's compressed lips. 'Say it, Tash. Whatever it is you want to say.'

Tasha groaned. 'I hate this. All the time I've known you I've wondered why you never get involved with men.' She flapped a hand. 'You can't count Maurice. I'm talking about relationships. Now I know the reason, and I can't do anything about it.'

'No one can, Tash. It's a mess.'

'My oath it is.' Tasha sniffed. 'I'm glad you told me, though. At least I can be here for you when he leaves. When will that be?"

Beth hesitated. 'I don't know. Soon, I expect. He doesn't have much more to do.'

As Tasha squeezed her hand again, Beth looked up. She wanted to ask her friend's advice. Should she give in to her aching desire to be with Pierre for the short time he was here? Or would it leave her open to heartbreak from which she'd never recover?

She couldn't do it. Whatever happened between them now—if anything—it was nobody's business but theirs.

'I'd better go,' she said. 'I've left Pierre looking at some figures in the office.'

'The review's going well, isn't it?'

'Yes.' She smiled. At least *that* was working out the way she'd hoped. She was confident he wouldn't be able to fault her figures, and now he'd opened his mind to her way of looking at the business she had every reason to hope she'd keep her winery.

The door of the office was wide open, so Pierre wasn't alerted to her approach. She stood in the doorway, watching him as he concentrated, his eyes darting between two sheets of figure-filled paper. For the first time since his arrival she allowed herself to enjoy the sight of him. To soak up the pleasure of seeing him here, at her winery.

She enjoyed it so much she felt completely light-headed. Her body simply couldn't cope with the amount of love flowing through her at this moment.

From the furrow between his eyebrows to the slight shadow of stubble along his jawline—everything about him etched itself into her mind, her heart. She would carry this image with her when he'd gone. And he *would* be gone, some day soon.

And suddenly she knew the answer to her dilemma. The time she had with him was limited. All the more reason to make the most of it. Better to have loved and lost...the saying went. She would well and truly test the truth of it.

She straightened, and the movement caught his eye. He looked up from the paperwork and smiled.

'You've done a thorough job on this forecast, Beth.'

'Don't call me that,' she said, moving into the room.

'What?'

'Call me Babette.' She walked around the desk and crouched beside him. 'I've missed hearing you say it.'

'My sweet Babette,' he said, taking her face gently between his hands. He sighed, stroking the pads of his thumbs across her cheeks. 'You sound tired.'

'I am. I haven't been sleeping well.'

He kissed the tip of her nose. 'So, what's next?'

'We could go back to the house and...see what happens.'

He grinned. 'I meant which of your innovative plans were you going to show me next. But never mind.'

He stood and, taking her hand, tugged her upright with him.

'Oh.' Beth leaned her head against his chest. 'Well, there's the olive oil…'

'Ah.'

'We could drive down to the olive grove. Production starts soon.'

'Tell me about it tomorrow.' He looped an arm around her shoulders. 'Your other idea was better.'

Beth awoke in her bed, but couldn't remember getting into it. The morning light filled her room and, glancing at the clock, she saw it was around her normal wake-up time. Then, as she rolled over, she realised she was fully clothed. Except for her shoes, she had on everything she'd worn the day before.

A picture of Pierre formed in her head, and she recalled falling asleep on his lap the night before, curled into his chest like a child. No wonder she'd slept so well. It wasn't what she'd intended. When they'd returned to the house she'd cooked dinner, but after she'd yawned her way through the eating of it Pierre had pulled her down onto the sofa and stroked her hair till… She couldn't remember anything else.

She smiled and hugged her pillow to her. He must have carried her to bed, and the thought of it made her belly tingle.

At a knock on the door, she jumped. It was a sound she'd never heard before. She called out to Pierre, and the door swung open. He entered carrying a tray.

'Breakfast,' he said, with the warmest smile she'd

seen in years. It melted the lump of ice she'd called her heart in recent times. She gave him one to match.

Wriggling into a sitting position, and tucking the cotton sheet around her, she peered over the edge of the tray.

'Toast,' he said. 'Is it all right? It's the best I could manage.'

'Perfect.'

He placed the tray across her legs and sat on the edge of the bed. 'How are you today?'

'I feel fantastic,' she said. 'I had the best sleep I've had for ages. Years.' She took a slice of toast from the plate and gave him a sheepish grin. 'Did you put me to bed?'

'Yes.' His eyes held a seductive glint. 'But that's all I did. When I make love to you, you're going to be awake.'

She inhaled a toast crumb and choked. He slapped her back, then rubbed it in circles till she calmed down.

'Drink some tea,' he said, handing a cup to her. 'I remember you would never drink coffee early in the morning.'

She sighed as she took the cup from him. He remembered the little things. Was it possible to burst with happiness? If only this could last—

No. She chopped off the thought. She wouldn't waste time on it. She'd made her decision. For the time they had, she was going to live in the present. She was going to enjoy it to the max. She was going to build a store of memories that would allow her to face the future alone.

'So, why did you plant olive trees on land you could have used for vines?'

At his sudden question she felt a twinge of defensiveness, but clamped down on it. It was a legitimate question, and he had every right to ask it. Swallowing a mouthful of toast, she said, 'We didn't plant them. The olive trees were already there.'

'Oh?'

She drank some tea. 'My father inherited them when he bought the property, but didn't see any value in them so he ignored them and they grew wild. Since I had the idea of harvesting the fruit and producing oil, Clive has worked very hard to bring the area under control. He's done a good job.'

Pierre turned his gaze to the window and was silent for a moment. 'You like Clive?'

'Of course I do. I like all my staff. They're the nearest thing I have to a family.' She shrugged. 'Jenny and Clive are great people. You'll like them.'

He grimaced. 'I will try not to be jealous of him.'

'Jealous?' She chuckled. 'Oh, it's nice to have someone to be jealous over me.' She flopped back against the pillows and gave him a dreamy smile. 'But why?'

'He has everything going for him. Looks, height, muscles. And…he lives here. Once I've left, he'll still be here.'

She stared at him. 'Seriously, don't be jealous of Clive. For one thing, he's married. His wife is a good friend of mine. I wouldn't dream of… The idea is ridiculous and…'

She fell silent.

'And?'

'And…I don't want him. There's only one man I want.'

Their gazes locked and held. A moment later she squealed. She hadn't seen him slip his hand under the sheet, and when it touched her foot her stomach leapt into her chest. He caressed her ankle, and she thought her bones would liquefy with the heat generated by his gentle touch.

'Oh,' she murmured, and she slid a little further down the pillows.

Her ankle chain strained against her skin as he slid his fingertips beneath it. In a flash, the memory of that day—the day he'd fastened the chain around her ankle—returned, and her whole body tingled. She looked into his darker-than-ever eyes and knew he remembered it too. For several moments they stared at each other. Then Pierre spoke, his tone tender, his voice almost a whisper.

'You still wear it?'

'Yes,' she said. 'Always.'

He cleared his throat. 'I saw it.' With his fingers on her ankle, he traced circles as he spoke, sending tantalising shudders the length of her leg. 'The day you were talking to Clive in your office I saw it, and knew it was the same one.'

She nodded. 'It's the same one. I could never bring myself to take it off. It would have been like cutting you out of my heart. And I couldn't do that either.'

She saw him take a deep breath before removing his hand. He leaned forward to place a delicate kiss on her lips, then stood and left the room.

She watched him go, before closing her eyes. Her mind raced—and as for her body... Well, everything seemed to be in working order. And she had wondered. On the rare occasions Maurice had tried to get physical her reaction had been less than lukewarm, whereas Pierre made her hot with the slightest touch. She burned for him.

CHAPTER THIRTEEN

'WHAT did you think of my profit forecast for the farm properties?' Beth asked Pierre on the short car journey to the olive grove, trying to make her mind work through the fog of her awareness of him. She saw the corners of his mouth twitch.

'I did a thorough risk assessment for the project. Remind me to show you later,' he said, in a serious tone.

'Oh.' She tapped the steering wheel. 'Don't make me wait till then. What was the result?'

'Ah.' He scratched his chin, as if trying to bring it to mind.

'Well?'

He grinned. 'Babette, I think you have a brilliant business brain.'

'Really?'

Tears sprang to her eyes. She tried to blink them away, but failed. She pulled the car over to the side of the road and parked on the loose gravel.

'What's wrong?' he asked.

'I can't see.' She dug in the pocket of her shorts for

a tissue, dabbed her eyes and blew her nose. 'It's the nicest thing anyone's ever said to me.'

He put an arm around her shoulders and pulled her towards him. 'But you didn't need anyone to tell you, did you? You knew.'

'Yes…no. I don't know.' She sobbed into his shoulder for a minute or two while he held her, then she took a deep breath and sat up straight. 'I'm fine now. I just wish my father could have heard you say it. And I wish he could see me trying to take good care of his dream.'

Pierre placed a tender kiss on her forehead. 'I am sure he knew you would.'

'Did he, though? Or did he just ask me because I was the only family he had?'

Pierre frowned. 'You have to stop thinking that way. From all I've heard, your father was an intelligent man. He must have known the kind of person you were. He must have known what you were capable of.'

'But after I let him down, he couldn't have known how much I cared. I wish I'd told him how proud of him I was, and how much Lowland Wines means to me because it's his legacy.'

He pulled her into his chest and rocked her while she let the last of her tears run down her face. She'd barely cried when her father died—had rarely cried over anything in the last ten years—but with Pierre back in her life it seemed she couldn't stop. After a while, she sniffed and sat up again.

'You really think I have a brilliant business brain?'

He nodded.

'That's a big turnaround from when you first arrived.'

He grimaced. 'I admit it. I was looking at the situation from a predetermined standpoint. I was wrong, and I apologise.'

She smiled. 'Apology accepted.'

'Would you like me to drive?'

She shook her head. 'We're nearly there, and my tears have all gone.' She gave her nose one last blow, then restarted the engine. 'Pierre?'

'Yes?'

'Now you know I have a—"brilliant business brain", are you going to make a positive report to the Board about my business plan?'

'So far I have seen nothing to justify doing otherwise.'

She grinned. 'That's a yes?'

'That's a yes.'

Laughing, she steered the car onto the road again. She was almost there. So close to having what she wanted. But it came at a price. At the expense of a future without Pierre.

They spent a short but information-packed time at the olive grove, after which they started back to the winery. Beth explained she had to be back to meet a tour bus of Japanese tourists.

'Is this a regular thing?' Pierre asked.

'It will be. This is the first one we've arranged so far. It's a private tour of the winery with a Japanese-speaking guide. I'm going to tag along on the first few, until our guide feels comfortable she has the answers to all possible questions.'

His eyes widened. 'These tours are also in your business plan, I assume?'

'Yes, and, based on my research, they will be quite lucrative. We arrange them through a Japanese travel agent, and the guide is John McGill's daughter, who's studied in Japan. I've hired her on a casual basis, so there's very little expense involved.'

'Excellent.'

She smiled. 'Again, I have the details to back up the forecast.'

He nodded. 'Of course you do.'

'And I think that's about it. We've covered everything in my business plan—except for the website.'

He frowned. 'The website makes money?'

'It's designed to keep our current customers informed, with the added aim of encouraging them to buy wine on a regular basis. It's not rocket science.' She smiled across at him. She loved being able to talk to him about the business in this frank, open manner. She loved sharing it with him. 'What will you do while I'm busy with the tour?'

He returned her smile. 'I think it's time to write my report. And, before you ask again, I promise it will be a positive one. Trust me.'

'I'm relieved. Thrilled.'

She gazed across the Lowland vines, straining under the weight of grapes ready for the upcoming vintage. She'd be there to see the next vintage, and many, many more. She'd have a chance to make the winery into something her father would have been proud of. Her imagination soared.

'Okay if I work in your office?'

Pierre's words brought her back to earth and she nodded. 'Sure. No problem. I'll meet you at the house this evening for dinner.'

That evening, Beth had just changed into a cool cotton dress when she heard Pierre open the front door. She ran her fingers through her hair, still damp from the shower, and left it to dry naturally. As she opened the bedroom door, Pierre turned to look at her. His expression warmed as his gaze travelled over the short dress, and she grinned at his reaction.

'Hot, isn't it?'

He nodded. 'An understatement. And as for the weather… Do I have time for a shower before dinner?'

'Sure.'

He continued to stare at her for a moment, before sighing and entering his room. Beth headed for the kitchen and heard the shower start up as she reached for some salad vegetables from the crisper.

So much had happened in a couple of days. Such a short time ago she'd been terrified of losing the winery and angry with Pierre. Now, she felt secure in the knowledge that he supported her plans, and her feelings for him were as far from anger as they could be.

She glanced out of the window and paused at the sight of a grey kangaroo grazing on the lawn. As she watched, a joey poked its head out of the pouch. What a shame, she thought, that Pierre would miss this. She hesitated for a moment, then dashed to the bathroom door. As she raised her hand to knock, the door opened and Pierre appeared, tucking in the end of a towel he'd draped around his hips.

His eyes widened. 'Babette? Is there a problem?'

'No, but there's something here you might find interesting.' She pointed towards the kitchen. 'Come and see.'

She hurried back to the kitchen, thinking that she'd just seen something interesting too. Pierre, wearing only a towel and with his hair wet, was the most interesting thing she'd seen in years.

'What is it?' he asked as he entered the kitchen behind her.

Pleased to see the roo still there, she pointed through the window. The joey had climbed out of the pouch, and looked cute with its sweet face and huge feet. She smiled up at Pierre.

'I thought it might be the first kangaroo you'd seen outside a zoo. It would be nice for you to tell Philippe about it.'

He gazed out of the window. 'Oh, yes. He'll love to hear about this.'

Beth allowed her own gaze to wander, and took note of his firm, muscled torso. The towel rested low on his hips, low enough to expose an arrow of dark hair, hinting at what it hid. She watched, entranced, as a trickle of water ran down his neck and meandered slowly through the scattered dark hair on his chest.

'I'm glad you called me,' he said, jerking her out of her trance.

His voice rumbled through her, low and sexy, and she felt a blush rush up her throat into her cheeks. He'd caught her checking him out. He had to know what she'd been thinking.

He slipped an arm around her shoulders, and she started at the cool dampness of his hand on her hot skin. He turned her to face him and slid the fingers of both hands into her still-damp hair. He lifted it from her neck, then ran his fingers down and across her shoulders, and back up to cup her face.

Her body ached from being from so close to him. She was ready for his kiss. So ready. But he didn't kiss her. She stared at his slightly parted lips, wondering why, then raised her eyes to look into his. They radiated desire. So what was he waiting for?

'Babette…' He sounded as if he'd swallowed gravel. 'You do know I can't stay here?'

'I know,' she whispered. 'And you know I can't leave.'

He nodded, leaning forward to touch his lips to her forehead. 'In spite of everything…do you still want me?'

She closed her eyes. Did she want him to take her to heights she'd never known since Paris? Oh, yes.

Did she want him to make her feel beautiful? Yes, definitely.

Did she want him to walk out of her life after they'd made love? No. But she'd made her choice. And she'd chosen to make the most of the time they had.

Her eyes fluttered open. 'I do.' She trailed her fingertips across his chest. 'I want you. I don't want to think about the future.'

He groaned, and gave in. His kiss was feather-light at first, and she sighed. Then he deepened it, and she knew it was the beginning of something dramatic and overwhelming. Something she'd wanted and needed for a very long time.

She ran her hands over the damp skin of his back, and felt a thrill when her touch made him suck in a breath. He caught her hands and kissed each palm before dropping them to her sides. He caressed her shoulders and nuzzled the sensitive skin where her shoulder curved into her neck. She whimpered, and he slid his fingers under the shoestring straps, easing them off her shoulders, lowering the light cotton fabric till he could kiss the curve of her breasts. She couldn't tell who groaned loudest.

'Oh, Pierre,' she said, her voice cracking as tears started to run down her cheeks. 'I've missed you so much.'

'Shh. Don't cry.' He made soothing noises while he kissed along her cheekbone, down her throat, across her collarbone.

'I can't stop.' Her voice broke on a sob.

He pulled back and took her hands in his. 'Babette, I understand. It's too much. It's overwhelming.'

Tugging her dress up to cover her breasts, he said. 'We shouldn't do this. It will be too difficult for you…afterwards.'

'No.' She smiled through her tears. 'We've waited so long. Let's not waste any more precious time.'

'Are you sure?'

'Completely.'

He gathered her against him and she arched her body into his. 'I don't want to have any regrets.'

CHAPTER FOURTEEN

WHEN Beth opened her eyes, the room was dark, and it took her a moment to register what had happened. She felt complete. Content. She held her breath as she stretched one foot tentatively across the bed, and sent up a silent prayer of thanks when it touched a warm body.

'I'm still here,' Pierre murmured.

More relieved than she could have said, she rolled onto her side and grinned at him as her eyes adjusted to the dim light.

'So you are.'

She took enormous pleasure in the sight of his sleepy dark eyes. He'd made love to her as if it really mattered, and whatever happened she'd never forget it.

He stroked her cheek. 'You are so beautiful.'

'I'm amazed you still think so. I'm ten years older than the last time.'

'You're like the best Lowland wine…aged to perfection.'

She laughed. 'And more full-bodied?'

'Mmm. Just the right amount.' He drew her close. 'And there's definitely added complexity.' He kissed her.

She sighed. 'You've improved with age too,' she said with a teasing grin. 'And that was exactly the right place to touch me.'

He gave her a questioning look. 'Where?'

'In the kitchen.' She giggled.

'Ah, talking of the kitchen—I'm very hungry. What about you?'

'Too right.' She glanced at the clock on the bedside table. 'It's not too late to make dinner.'

She kissed him on the cheek, then hopped out of bed and gathered her undies and dress from the floor. Having slipped them on, she took a moment to watch Pierre climb out of bed, then followed him as he crossed the passageway to his room. He'd hardly changed, except for a small scar on his back. That was new. She could have sworn to it in a court of law, she remembered his body so well.

'How did you hurt your back?' she asked as he pulled on some boxer shorts.

He turned with a blank look.

'There's a scar that you didn't have before.'

'I'd forgotten.' He shrugged. 'A souvenir of Arlette.'

'What do you mean?'

He sighed. 'In the early years of our marriage she was very jealous. Very possessive.'

'But you said you didn't love each other.'

'No, I said *I* didn't love *her*. She did love me. In her own way. Unfortunately, every time I went away on business she was convinced I was flying to Australia.'

'To me?'

He nodded. 'She knew I wasn't over you. We argued about you a great deal. Almost constantly for a while.'

Her stomach flipped, and she squashed the perverse pleasure she felt, knowing there was more to the story. 'The scar?'

'She became more and more aggressive in our arguments. Then violent. The last time we argued, she had a knife…'

'Oh, my God. She stabbed you?'

He nodded. 'It was not a serious wound.'

'Bad enough to leave a scar.' She felt a surge of hatred for the woman who'd tried to make sure he could never return to her. But as her mind raced, hatred turned to concern for his son.

'If Arlette is violent,' she said, 'it's all the more reason to take Philippe away from her. That will be good for your case, surely? It makes it more likely you will win.'

'I don't believe he is in physical danger. I have never known her to raise a hand to him. She does not care enough about him to go to the trouble.'

Beth felt her heart twist in her chest. So what if it meant Pierre would have to live in France? She couldn't begrudge the boy his father. He deserved a parent who loved him and would give him a happy childhood. She would cope. She would have to.

Pierre had dressed in jeans and a loose T-shirt while they talked, and they went through to the kitchen together.

'Does Philippe like fish?' she asked.

He shrugged. 'I don't know.'

'Well, I'll show you a really simple meal you'll be able to make for him. Nutritious too.'

He climbed on to a bar stool and watched with interest as she quickly peeled two large potatoes and put them into water to boil. 'But you don't get away with doing nothing,' she said. 'While they're cooking, we need to chop the herbs.'

She took bunches of parsley, basil and rosemary from the fridge, and handed a large knife and a chopping board to Pierre. 'Your first practical cooking lesson.'

It took him a while to get the hang of chopping rather than slicing the herbs, but once he did he seemed to enjoy himself.

Beth finished preparing the tossed salad she'd started earlier, and under Beth's instructions Pierre drained and sliced the potatoes and placed them in a casserole, added the herbs and a can of chopped tomatoes, cut the fish into chunks and laid it on top.

'Now, there's only one more ingredient, and you should be able to guess what that is.'

He shrugged.

'It's the most important one,' she said with mock exasperation. She took a bottle of dry white wine from the fridge, poured a glassful, and tipped it into the casserole dish.

He chuckled. 'Of course. I should have known.'

'It will be cooked in fifteen to twenty minutes,' she said as she slid the dish into the oven. 'How easy was that?'

'Very.'

'Even for non-cooks like us.' Beth took the rest of the wine to the table.

Pierre carried the glasses.

'Is your report all finished now?' she asked.

'Yes. I've e-mailed it to Frank. As a matter of courtesy, I'll call him before I distribute it to the Board.'

'So now you've officially finished what you came here to do?'

He smiled. 'Yes.'

'You'll be able to relax tomorrow, then?'

'I suppose so. Why, what did you have in mind?'

'Nothing. I just think it will be good for you to have a holiday.'

'You could be right. I cannot remember the last time I had a holiday. And there is no place I would rather spend it.'

The next morning, Beth leaned over and gave Pierre a lingering kiss on the lips.

'Mmm.' He rubbed his eyes. 'That was nice. What time is it?'

'It doesn't matter. You're on holiday.'

He blinked at her. 'What about you?'

'I'm going to the office to do the banking. If I don't, no one will get paid. Thank God for the internet.'

'How long will it take?'

'A couple of hours. Then we can do anything you want for the rest of the day.'

He raised his eyebrows. 'Anything?'

'Within reason.' She laughed. 'You have a couple of hours to think up something.'

He sat up and reached for her, but she dodged his hand.

'No, I really must go, or my staff might go on strike.'

'Okay, but will you do me a favour?'

'Sure. What?' She let her eyes roam over his bare

chest while she waited. A pulsing reaction started up in the pit of her stomach, and she had to look away before she changed her mind about going to the office at all.

'Bring my laptop back with you. I left it on your desk.'

'Sure.'

'And come back quickly.'

'No problem.' She blew him a kiss from the door.

Nearly two hours later, Beth shut down the computer and stretched her arms above her head to release the tension in her shoulders. Moving across to Pierre's computer, she disconnected it from the power outlet and smiled as she packed it away. With luck, he wouldn't need it again for a few days. It would be nice to see him relax. And it would be even nicer to relax with him.

As she reached down to the floor for the computer case, she caught sight of a pile of papers sitting face-up in the wastepaper bin. Pierre's handwriting. She smiled. Even after all the time that had passed she'd recognise it anywhere. In their younger days he'd written her cute little notes before he'd worked up the nerve to tell her how he felt. Without giving a thought to what she was doing, she read the first few lines of the front page.

It immediately became clear that the pages were Pierre's notes for his report. She dragged her eyes away. She'd only read one paragraph, but it was obvious he'd been true to his word. If the rest of the report was anything like the beginning, the directors would have to give her a chance. What else could they do? They'd asked an expert for his opinion and he'd given it, in no uncertain terms.

A warm glow spread through her. She'd only been away for a couple of hours, but already she missed him. She couldn't wait to see him again. Zipping up his computer case, she headed out of the office.

On the way back to the house, she wondered what he'd dreamed up for the afternoon. She really didn't mind. As long as they were together, she would be happy to do whatever he wanted—go out or, better still, stay in.

She pushed open the front door and made for the kitchen, drawn by the aroma of percolating coffee. But as she passed the door to Pierre's room she turned her head and saw him.

Packing.

Panic gripped her, and she forced herself to stay calm though the bottom was threatening to fall out of her world. She moved into the doorway and leaned against the frame.

'What are you doing?'

Startled, Pierre looked up. 'Babette, I...' He dropped a pile of clothes into the suitcase and stepped towards her, reaching for her.

She stepped back. 'What are you doing?' she asked again, her voice wavering.

He let his hands drop. 'I have to go.'

'Already?'

'I've spoken to my lawyer. He's been trying to contact me. Because my assistant has been away, his message went astray.' His face twisted. 'I have to get back to France urgently. We're due in court in a couple of days for the custody hearing.'

She drew in a sharp breath, trying to fill the growing emptiness inside her.

'This is it. This is the chance I've been waiting for. I can't…' He turned away, moving back to the bed to finish his packing. 'I can't miss it.'

'No, of course you can't.' Her voice sounded steadier this time. Steadier than she felt. 'Have you booked a flight?'

He nodded as he flipped the lid of the case closed.

'Right. Well, I don't think I'll hang around to watch you go.'

'Babette.' He stepped towards her again, and once more she moved back.

'Don't, Pierre.'

'You knew…' He pushed a hand through his hair. 'We both knew this would happen.'

'Yes.' She chewed on her bottom lip for a moment, struggling to overcome the growing emptiness inside her. 'But not so soon. I thought we'd have some time together before it happened. I thought I'd have time to prepare for this.'

He gave a helpless shrug. 'I don't know what to say.'

'Don't say anything. I'm going back to my office. You'll be gone when I get back?'

'I've ordered a taxi.'

She took a deep breath and exhaled slowly, her eyes fixed on the floor. 'That's it then.' She turned and strode to the front door.

Pierre followed her. 'I'll call you.'

'No.' She paused with her hand on the doorknob and turned back slowly. 'Please don't make this harder than it has to be.'

'We can keep in touch. There will be holidays and—'

'No, Pierre. I can't spend my life waiting for a phone call from you, surviving on a week or two a year. How can you even ask me to do that?'

She tugged open the door and lurched through. 'It would be better to have…a clean break…'

She half-ran, half-staggered along the track, trying not to think, to keep her mind blank till she reached the sanctuary of her office. Once there, she locked the door, crossed to the window and, with a groan, slumped to the floor. With her forearms on the windowledge and her head resting on them, she cursed fate for allowing her only one beautiful, special night before taking him away from her.

But at least she had that one night to hold on to. Even through her heartbreak she knew she would always be grateful for that. For the memory of one night. For the opportunity to see, to feel how much he loved her.

Heartbroken as she'd been when she'd lost Pierre all those years ago, this was infinitely worse—because she knew exactly what was happening. She wasn't a bewildered nineteen-year-old. She was a grown woman, and she'd made her choice. As he had. They'd both put other priorities ahead of their own needs.

A chill seeped through her, taking the place of her blood, leaving her frozen and weak. She'd never know love again. Would never know the joy of being in the arms of the man she loved. She'd never even told him how much she loved him. The ground seemed to shake beneath her, shattering the beautiful illusion that had been her life since the day of their picnic, pitching her into a black hole.

CHAPTER FIFTEEN

PIERRE knew from experience that no amount of alcohol would make him feel better. He called the waiter back to the table and changed his order to a mineral water. No point in trying to drown his sorrows when he knew they would last for years. Nothing would make him forget her. Nothing had worked before. And he didn't need to make a fool of himself by getting drunk.

He scanned the dinner menu but couldn't focus on the names of the dishes. Taking a calming breath, he started at the top again. He had to aim for normality to get through this. And normality meant eating regularly and behaving as though everything was fine. One day at a time. He could do it. He was an expert at it.

He made his selection and snapped the menu shut. What a damned nuisance he hadn't been able to fly out of the country this afternoon. Of all the times for the airport's computer system to crash, grounding all flights until morning. The fact that it was a newly built airport was no excuse. Now he had to mark time till morning, with nothing to do but think. The very thing he did not want to do.

The waiter arrived at the table to take his food order, and he had to open the menu again. He'd forgotten what he'd chosen. He pointed at one of the items and the young man scribbled on a pad.

As he closed the menu, he heard a tinkly laugh from another table. He looked up sharply. *Not her.* He knew it before he saw the brunette responsible for twisting his insides. The woman caught his eye and smiled. He didn't smile back.

What had he done to deserve this? Was he such a bad person that the fates wanted to punish him? Why did he always have to choose between the people and the things that he loved?

Was it wrong to want the woman he cared so deeply for and the son he adored to both be in his life at the same time? He didn't think so. But he'd had to choose. Just as he'd had to choose between Beth and his family's winery.

He wasn't one to rail against fate normally. What he couldn't change, he accepted, and when he *could* change something he went all out to do what had to be done.

He looked up as the waiter delivered his food. He didn't even recognise what was on his plate. Not that it mattered. He couldn't eat it.

This was one case where there was nothing he could do. He simply had to accept what life had dished up to him.

Or did he?

A spark of an idea ignited in his mind. He glanced at his watch. With the time difference, his lawyer would be in his office now. He rose to his feet, catching the chair as it fell, and headed for his room.

* * *

'Beth?' Tasha peered around the office door, eyebrows raised.

'I'm alone,' Beth said, grimacing at the stark truth of her statement.

Tasha walked in, frowning and clutching a large manila envelope against her chest. 'Has Pierre left?'

'Yes.'

'Is he coming back?'

Beth shook her head.

'Is that why you look dreadful this morning?

She nodded. She'd sat in her office for hours. Not working, just staring into space. After a while, she'd known she should go home, but she hadn't moved. She couldn't face walking into her house, where she would smell him—his distinctive aftershave, the coffee he'd made. She'd see reminders right through the house— from the bed he'd used to the extra towel in the bathroom. She wasn't ready to face all that.

When she had eventually forced herself to go home, she hadn't been able to sleep. For a long time she'd lain curled in a foetal position on the bed, dry-eyed, paralysed by grief. At some stage during the night she'd undressed and crawled into bed, but it had been almost dawn before tears began to flow and she'd cried herself to sleep.

But today was another day, and she had put all the tears and regrets behind her. The pain in her chest might mock that claim, but she had no intention of digging them up again to share with Tasha. The future was her winery. As long as she had it, it would be her life. Nothing else mattered.

Tasha's face showed her sympathy. 'Oh, sweetie. Do you want a shoulder to cry on?'

Beth took a deep breath. 'You know what? I'm all cried out. I don't think I could squeeze out another tear, even for you.'

Tasha sat down opposite Beth. 'At least talk about it. How do you feel?'

'Fine. It's nothing I can't handle.' She shuffled a pile of papers.

Tasha sighed. 'So you're shutting me out again?'

Beth's stomach turned over. 'No, Tash. It's not like that. I simply have to get through this the only way I can. By working. By devoting myself to fulfilling Dad's dream.'

'Well…' With a shrug, Tasha leaned forward. 'If you change your mind, I'll be waiting. In the meantime, I thought something must have happened, because I found this envelope shoved under the door this morning.' She tapped the large manila envelope with a bright red fingernail. 'And there's a note stuck to it.'

She peeled the yellow sticky paper from the envelope as she spoke. 'Pierre wants me to give it to you. I wondered why he didn't do it himself.'

'Oh, right. Must be his report.' Beth held out her hand for the envelope. She slit it and removed several stapled sheets, plus a memo from Pierre as a cover page. She scanned the list of addressees, and then the subject line. All as expected.

'Thanks, Tash,' she said, putting the report aside. 'I'll catch up with you at lunchtime, okay?'

Tasha hesitated. 'You sure you'll be all right?'

Beth managed a weak smile. 'Sure.'

Once Tasha had left, Beth heaved a sigh, positioned the report in front in her, leaned her elbows on the desk and began to read.

It was not merely a good report, but a glowing testimonial. Pierre couldn't have done more to ensure her position if he'd held the directors at gunpoint. If they turfed her out now, it would be for some reason other than a lack of belief in her ability. And they wouldn't do it, she was sure.

Contrary to her earlier statement, a solitary tear trickled down one cheek. He could have written a lousy report, ensuring she'd lose her job. Then she wouldn't have had a choice to make. She could have gone to live in France with him and his son.

She fought a choking sensation, pushed away the report and studied her shaking hands. She thrust them into her hair for the sake of doing something with them. Pierre had too much integrity to do something like that.

She grabbed the telephone in one hand, then shook her head at the stupid urge to ring him. He wouldn't even be in France yet. The flight took longer than this. She replaced the handset firmly. And when he did arrive the last thing she should do was ring him. She'd been right when she'd said a clean break was the best way to go. If only it wasn't so damned difficult.

She stood and walked to the window. Here was her favourite view and, after all the anguish she'd gone through it would remain hers.

Not long now and the vivid green vines would be transformed into brown heavily pruned stumps. With the vintage just around the corner, life would be hectic. She wouldn't have a minute to think about Pierre. She hoped.

As in previous years, the whole community would be involved. She'd fought tooth and nail to save this community, and she'd won. It was a good feeling. And she would be rewarded when she saw her friends and neighbours come together to celebrate another successful vintage.

If only…

She closed her eyes and clenched her muscles. There was no point in wishing Pierre could be there to experience it with her, because it simply wouldn't happen. She'd never see Pierre again.

After a pain-filled moment, her eyes drifted open and she stared out of the window. A white taxicab wound its way towards the winery, and she wondered vaguely whether it contained tourists on the lookout for a wine tasting. Tasha would look after them. She shifted her gaze to the hills and let her eyes become unfocused while she contemplated what she should do next.

Hearing the creaking hinges of her office door, she blinked rapidly to clear the remains of tears from her eyes before turning to face…

'Pierre?'

It was really him. Standing in her office. Large as life.

'I don't understand.'

Judging from the dark circles under his eyes, he hadn't slept any better than she had.

'I need to talk to you,' he said. He moved forward till he was only an arm's length from her, but he didn't touch her.

His urgent tone awoke something inside her. She hardly dared hope, but something important had happened.

She swallowed, looking into his eyes, as deep and dark as mine shafts, staring back at her. 'What is it?'

'What I did wrong last time was to let you go without a fight. Without asking for what I wanted.'

'Yes.' It came out as a whisper.

'Not this time. It took me a long time to learn my lesson, but I've learned it. I will not make the same mistake again.'

Beth could only wait for him to go on. She didn't have the strength left to question him.

'What I want is to have both you *and* Philippe in my life. Is that too much to ask?'

'But I can't leave—'

'No. You can't leave Lowland Wines. I know it. I understand completely. So…'

'So…?'

'So I had an idea. I thought, if I offered Arlette enough money, she might give up custody of Philippe voluntarily. I don't know why it never occurred to me before. But desperate times… It seems I have been inspired by your lateral thinking.' He smiled wearily. 'I've been on the phone all night with my lawyer while he made her the offer.'

Beth sucked in a breath. 'Did she accept?'

'She nearly bit off his hand.' He grunted. 'She has committed to signing a formal agreement. It specifies that she will agree to me taking Philippe out of the country. To live.'

He reached out a hand and stroked a finger down her cheek. The heat in his eyes made her bones melt. 'I want to bring him here,' he said. 'If you agree. I want him to grow up in the Barossa Valley and have the kind of childhood I had, around people who care about each other and help each other. And I want him to live with his brothers and sisters.'

She fell against his chest, smothering a sob. She wouldn't cry now. Not when she was about to have everything she could possibly want.

Pressed close to his chest, she could feel his heart hammering, and she smiled. It was good to know he was as strongly affected as her. Lifting her head, she grinned up at him. 'How many brothers and sisters?'

'How many do you want?'

'Well, let's start with one and see how we go.'

'We could start that one now. There's time before I leave for the airport.' He checked his wristwatch.

'You're still going?'

'I have to. To sign the agreement. I want to get it done as soon as possible.'

She nodded, unable to speak for the joy that filled her heart to near bursting.

He shrugged, then pulled her back into his chest. 'Why did it take us so long to work this out? Other people meet, fall in love, get married. Why has it taken us so long to reach this point?'

'Well, when we first met we were young—'

'But I knew what I wanted. And I was right. I knew I would always love you. Nothing has changed.'

Beth nodded slowly. 'I never stopped loving you, Pierre. And I never will.'

They kissed till they were both breathless, and Beth pulled back to look into his face.

'Are you are going to ask me to marry you?'

'I am. And even if you say no I'll never let you go again. Whatever happens.'

'Then I might as well marry you.' She kissed him on the lips. 'But what are you going to do about your job?'

'My job…?' He frowned, as if he'd lost the thread of the conversation.

'Your job. With L'Alliance.'

His face cleared. 'Ah, we haven't discussed…' He put her away from him and pushed a hand through his hair. 'Beth, if you want to, we should be able to organise a management buy-out.'

She gasped. 'Buy back Lowland Wines?' She stared. 'Are you serious?'

He nodded. 'I still have most of my half of the money from the sale of the Laroche winery, and can raise more if necessary. I believe your cousin Simon would like to be involved. Maybe Owen too. It would be a family winery again. And we could pass it on to our children.'

Tears filled her eyes.

'But only if you want to. It's *your* winery. I don't want you to think I would try to take over here.'

'I love the idea,' she said past the tightness in her throat. She'd give almost anything in the world to see her father's reaction, to see the pride shining in his eyes. She covered her mouth with a hand.

'Your father would be very proud of you,' he said, as if he'd read her thoughts. 'He'd be proud of what you've achieved, whether we succeed with this or not.'

Her heart swelled with love for him. 'We *will* succeed.'

And she could imagine nothing better than having

the ownership of Lowland Wines back where it belonged. Except for one thing—sharing it with Pierre. And their family.

In February, expect **MORE**
from

HARLEQUIN® *Romance*®

as it increases to six titles per month.

What's to come...

Rancher and Protector

Part of the

Western Weddings
miniseries

BY JUDY CHRISTENBERRY

The Boss's
Pregnancy Proposal

BY RAYE MORGAN

Don't miss February's
incredible line up of authors!

www.eHarlequin.com   HRINCREASE

nocturne™

WAS HE HER SAVIOR
OR HER NIGHTMARE?

HAUNTED
LISA CHILDS

Years ago, Ariel and her sisters were separated for
their own protection. Now the man who vowed
revenge on her family has resumed the hunt, and
Ariel must warn her sisters before it's too late.
The closer she comes to finding them, the more
secretive her fiancé becomes. Can she trust the man
she plans to spend eternity with? Or has he been
waiting for the perfect moment to destroy her?

On sale December 2006.

HARLEQUIN® Romance®

What a month!

In February watch for

Rancher and Protector
Part of the Western Weddings miniseries
BY JUDY CHRISTENBERRY

The Boss's Pregnancy Proposal
BY RAYE MORGAN

Also in February, expect
MORE of what you love
as the Harlequin Romance line
increases to six titles per month.

REQUEST YOUR FREE BOOKS!
2 FREE NOVELS PLUS 2
FREE GIFTS!

HARLEQUIN ROMANCE®

From the Heart, For the Heart

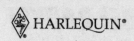
Coming Next Month

#3931 RANCHER AND PROTECTOR Judy Christenberry
Western Weddings

Rancher Jason Barton is all business and steely glares! Rosie Wilson has recently had a run of bad luck—but she's a fighter, and she means business, too. When they get stranded under the starlit Western sky, there's only one place Rosie wants to be: in the arms of the cowboy who has vowed to protect her.

#3932 THE VALENTINE BRIDE Liz Fielding
The Brides of Bella Lucia

Louise Valentine has been offered a job, and Max Valentine wants to help her save the family business. But since discovering she is adopted, Louise is not feeling charitable toward the Valentines. Sparks fly and soon they are both falling hard—will the past stand in the way of a special Valentine wedding?

#3933 ONE SUMMER IN ITALY... Lucy Gordon

It was supposed to be just a holiday... But then, enchanted by the pleading eyes of a motherless little girl and her brooding, enigmatic father, Matteo, Holly is swept away to their luxurious villa. Soon Holly discovers Matteo is hiding some dark secrets—her one summer in Italy is only the beginning....

#3934 THE BOSS'S PREGNANCY PROPOSAL Raye Morgan

Working for her heart-stoppingly handsome boss shouldn't have been hard for Callie, but then he asks her to have a baby with him! Of course, love wouldn't come into the arrangement—as a busy CEO, Grant wants a family, but he's been hurt before. Could sensible Callie be just what he's looking for?

#3935 CROWNED: AN ORDINARY GIRL Natasha Oakley

Just as Prince Sebastian caught a glimpse of normal life, the untimely death of his father, the King of Andovaria, forced him to leave behind his most precious gift—the love of an ordinary girl. Now, years later, Marianne Chambers is in town. Can Seb fight tradition and claim her as his very own princess?

#3936 OUTBACK BABY MIRACLE Melissa James
Heart to Heart

As untamed as the Outback land he masters, cattleman Jake Connors is a mystery to Laila. Something about him calls to her in a way no other man has. But before he can give her his heart, Jake must stop running from the demons of his past. Might Laila's pregnancy surprise be the miracle they both need?